MONSTER'S REWARD

BLACKTHORN ACADEMY FOR SUPERNATURALS

BOOK EIGHT

PEPPER MCGRAW

NAUGHTY NIGHTS PRESS LLC• CANADA

Monster's Reward

Blackthorn Academy for
Supernaturals
Book Eight
Copyright © 2023
Pepper McGraw
ISBN: 978-1-77357-593-3
978-1-77357-594-0
Published by Naughty Nights Press LLC
Edited By JL Troughton
Cover Art By Silvana G. Sánchez
@ SelfPub Designs

MONSTER'S REWARD

Victim. Killer. Shadow Monster.

Kasima Smith grew up in human foster care, without any knowledge of her birth family or her origins. Then her monster emerges in a moment of extreme peril and her life is changed forever. Now a student at Blackthorn Academy, she's tasked with keeping her head down and learning how to somehow control the monster inside.

To make matters worse, she's forbidden from using her newly discovered shadow skills because as it turns out, she's the only monster of her kind left in the world and will be hunted if she's discovered alive. Then, she realizes fellow student,

MONSTER'S REWARD

Jahrdran Vilnik, is hunting her. Whether it's because he plans to kill her or claim her as his mate is anyone's guess.

Blackthorn Academy may not survive the shadows or the chaos that Kasi brings with her.

Monster's Reward is book eight in the Blackthorn Academy for Supernaturals shared world, featuring sexy, possessive monsters, sassy heroines, shadow-kitten familiars, and more.

CHAPTER ONE

A MONSTER WAS born the night I was attacked.

Maybe the monster always lived inside me, I don't know.

All I know is I wasn't aware of her before the attack, but she is always there now, scraping at my skin, begging for release.

The night it happened, there was a thundering in my ears as two men held me down on the ground while another ripped at my blouse—men, who let's be clear, are the *real* monsters of this tale—when she was born.

She exploded from me in streams of darkness, tentacles made only of shadow and mist that settled over the men and slowly devoured them.

I can still hear their screams.

Not that I feel any guilt over their deaths. They deserved far worse as far as I was concerned, especially since their deaths caused me a whole host of new problems.

Like derailing my entire life when Blackthorn Academy came for me.

The headmistress sent her dean of students to *invite* me to attend their academy, and by invite, I mean, inform me of my mandatory enrollment, starting right fucking then.

I had no interest in going back to school.

Been there, done that, got the high school diploma to prove it.

School sucked.

But here was this man, this *Professor Edwin Dunlop,* telling me I had no choice. I had to go to Blackthorn Academy to learn to control my monster blah-blah-blah.

Color me *not* impressed.

Unfortunately, according to the Professor, it was Blackthorn Academy or prison for supernaturals, since after all, my monster had killed three men.

I tried to point out there was absolutely no evidence of this (there wasn't even a single drop of blood at the scene of the supposed crime), but apparently, innocent until proven guilty isn't a thing in the supernatural community.

So back to school I went.

Here's the thing though.

Blackthorn Academy was like no other school I had ever attended.

And given I'd been in the human foster care system my entire life, I'd attended a *lot* of different schools through the years. In fact, I'd celebrated the acquisition of my diploma with a vow to never darken the doors of any educational institution again.

Fast forward three years and keeping that vow meant going to prison.

So that's how I ended up an

indentured student, *again,* this time held hostage by Blackthorn Academy until I could prove my ability to control my monster.

It wasn't all bad.

The classes were occasionally interesting and the professors were helpful, more or less.

They were also a tiny bit afraid of me, something they couldn't hide no matter how hard they tried, and something my monster reveled in.

She loved the scent of their fear any time we met in secret for those private lessons Headmistress Blackthorn deemed absolutely necessary.

Private because, according to her, my species—we were called shadow monsters—had been hunted to extinction hundreds of years before, which meant my existence was quite the mystery.

It was also, according to my professors, unlikely to last if anyone discovered my secret. The minute that happened, they assured me, I would be hunted.

None of them, however, would tell me *why*.

Were shadow monsters so terrible we actually *needed* exterminating, and if so, what on earth had I just become?

Unfortunately, these were questions my professors weren't prepared to answer, so I was left in the dark, even as I followed all their rules.

Which meant I attended classes like all the other students, but wasn't allowed to use any of my shadow skills in front of them. In other words, I appeared utterly incompetent.

I honestly wouldn't care except it also made me a potential target for bullies, something I absolutely could not allow to happen given my monster's propensity for violent revenge.

So, I spent the majority of my first year gritting my teeth and ignoring the whispers and snide comments, while developing my ability to blend into the shadows so that no one noticed me.

By the end of that year, most students had completely forgotten I even existed, which as far as I was concerned, was a good thing, especially since I was constantly hiding from *him*.

The beast who hunted me.

MONSTER'S REWARD

And eventually, the beast I used the shadows to stalk.

Let's be clear. I'm not *proud* that I've become a stalker, but once I discovered how easy it was to follow him around, I just couldn't resist.

I blame Professor Pulmeyer, who had me contemplating new ways to use the shadows in her Magical Transportation class.

I'm sure she didn't intend for me to learn what I did in that class.

It's just that I found the *concept* of magical transportation way more interesting than the *reality* of using mirrors to do so.

After all, what if there were no mirrors nearby?

It seemed so limiting. It definitely

wouldn't allow me to follow my obsession around.

At that point, all I'd learned to do was blend into the shadows around me, the benefits of which could not be overstated, but how would I ever learn about my obsession if all I could do was hide and then watch him walk away?

When I enrolled in Professor Pulmeyer's Magical Transportation class my second year, though, all that changed.

Watching students slip from one side of a mirror to a location far from us, literally disappearing before our eyes, had me wondering whether I could do the same from the shadows.

After all, I'd become so adept at hiding in them, I'd become virtually invisible to my classmates, even when they were looking right at me. All I had to do now was maintain that invisibility while moving.

With this in mind, I began to experiment with movement while standing in the shadows. What I discovered was that I couldn't necessarily travel from the castle grounds (yes, the Academy was actually housed inside a real-live castle) to the nearby town of Wellspring, at least not all at once, but I *could* slip from one shadow to the next without being seen.

Theoretically, if there were enough shadows available, I might eventually be able to make it all the way to Wellspring if I tried. Not that I ever did. I was more interested in exploring the castle itself and discovering whatever secrets it housed, particularly any that pertained to my own history and the demise of my people.

I had always had an affinity for the shadows, even before my monster made her appearance, but now it was as if they were growing in my presence, constantly reaching out to me, sliding over me whenever I stood near them, enveloping me in their shroud of darkness.

And I liked it.

No, I *loved* it.

I spent more and more time in the shadows, sliding from one to the next, catching whispered conversations between students and teachers alike.

I had unwittingly become the keeper

of their secrets—some of them rather boring, but others quite shocking—and I had no one to share them with.

Until the day I dragged Jahrdran into the shadows with me.

CHAPTER TWO

JAHRDRAN VILNIK WAS my obsession, hence the stalking.

I've never actually met him in person, but trust me, he makes an impression.

I'd seen him for the first time at the end of my third day at the Academy, and in a way, he became the reason I discovered how sheltering the shadows could actually be for me.

I'd just reached the main floor, having

descended six flights of stairs, grumbling the entire way down, when a roar shook the floor and rattled the windows. This wasn't necessarily unusual at the academy, I'd discovered. Beasting-out was kind of a thing among the monsters at Blackthorn, but no other beast had instantly consumed my attention the way he did.

He exploded from a room not far from where I stood, let out another roar and started hunting.

There was no other word to describe it.

He lifted his snout to the air and inhaled, then whipped around to face me.

That was when I discovered the shadows were my safety zone.

They'd reached out the moment my adrenaline spiked and had wrapped around me, pulling me back into their comforting embrace.

I stared at the giant beast.

He stood upright on two legs, but that was where his humanity ended. He was covered in black fur with pointy, wolf-like ears on top of his head and eyes that glowed a brilliant blue.

He stared straight into the shadows and I stared back at him.

He scented the air several more times, before finally turning and loping away, stopping every few feet to turn around and stare down the corridor toward the shadows still wrapped around me.

It wasn't until later, after many such

encounters like this one, that I finally realized the shadows were not only hiding me, but also masking my scent.

Despite the fact that he was a year ahead of me, and therefore, wasn't in any of my classes, I was always watching for him, trying to catch a glimpse of his beast.

Whenever it happened, he seemed able to sense that I was near and would go hunting while I watched from the shadows, wondering if he would ever figure out where I was hiding and slide into the shadows with me.

So far, it hadn't happened.

That first year, the shadows were always empty, a reminder that I was the last of my kind and completely alone in the world.

Then, one day, not too long into my second year, I slid into the shadows and found a cat waiting there for me.

Not one of those house cats humans have deluded themselves into thinking they've domesticated.

No. This cat was feral and made entirely of darkness. She blended so well in the shadows that I didn't even notice her at first.

Then she let out a yowl of welcome and launched herself at me.

Though I hadn't expected her and didn't even really know what she was, I caught her in my arms and laughed softly, joy filling all the empty spaces where loneliness had lived for so long.

She nuzzled my neck, climbed up and over my shoulder, scrabbled down my back, around my waist and back up my torso to my opposite shoulder.

She then draped herself from my shoulder all the way down my right arm, wrapping herself around it, then settling deep, slowly fading from smoke to solid, inky lines until she lay dormant upon my skin.

From that moment on, she traveled with me everywhere, either somewhere on my body as an incredibly detailed tattoo or slinking from shadow to shadow as I walked in the real world.

And of course, whenever I slid into the shadows to travel or to watch Jahrdran, she was right there by my side.

Over time, I learned how to communicate with her.

PEPPER MCGRAW

In the beginning, she would send images to me, ones that arrived fully formed in my mind. Later, as I chatted with her more and more, those images began to be accompanied by a single word or phrase.

This was how I eventually learned her name.

She sent me an image of herself along with two words: Shadow Cat.

I don't know if that was the name of her species or her actual name, but I began calling her Shadow for short and she seemed to like the sound of it, letting out a roaring purr every time I said her name.

So, that was how I spent the first semester of my second year: bonding with Shadow, attending classes (still unnoticed by the other students), taking individual lessons from my professors (who now tended to freak out anytime they caught sight of Shadow), and occasionally being hunted by Jahrdran Vilnik.

There was one additional change that came about the minute Headmistress Blackthorn noticed my rather obvious tattoo. She immediately added Familiar Training to my already overloaded schedule.

When I tried to point out that Shadow wasn't a familiar, but simply my companion, Headmistress Blackthorn gave me one of her looks—the kind that says you're an idiot—and snapped, "And just what do you think a familiar is, Kasima Smith?"

I sighed. The Headmistress was the only adult who consistently used my full name, refusing to call me Kasi.

"Companions, ma'am?"

"Exactly."

So that was that.

Since Shadow was made of smoke and mist, she couldn't show herself in class without the risk of someone guessing my secret.

This meant I had to attend Familiar Training without a familiar, which just made me weirder and more incompetent in the eyes of my classmates.

It also meant I had to attend one-on-one lessons with Professor Dewar. This wasn't fun for any of us because as it turned out, she had a cat named Verity and Verity was not fond of Shadow Cats.

MONSTER'S REWARD

Anytime she caught sight of Shadow, she would immediately attempt to attack her, which only resulted in Shadow tormenting her.

Sometimes Shadow would go smokier and mistier than ever, causing Verity to slide right through her.

Other times, Shadow would simply disappear from whatever shadow she was standing in and reappear in a different one, causing Verity to bound from shadow to shadow, in a desperate bid to catch the bad kitty.

But what would *really* set Verity off was when Shadow would launch herself across the room and up onto my shoulder, where she'd stretch down across my arm in tattoo form.

From there, she would mostly lie

dormant except for her tail, which she would drape over the side and occasionally twitch Verity's way.

If that wasn't enough to get Verity going, Shadow would slowly peel her head away from my shoulder or my forearm just enough to bare a fang, lay back her ears, twitch her whiskers or any combination of the three before settling down again.

In the beginning, I was sure Verity would attempt to attack Shadow again—and by extension, *me*—and I'd end up with a shredded arm as a result, but instead, Verity would go on a tear around whatever room we happened to be in.

This usually resulted in a lot of damage as she raced around knocking things over.

Eventually, when Professor Dewar got tired of cleaning up all the damage, we started meeting outside in the professors' personal garden, a place students were usually forbidden to visit.

It was in this garden I learned how to bring things into the shadows with me, thus instigating my downfall.

It was all Professor Dewar's fault.

Well, hers and Professor Pulmeyer's, who taught me how to move from shadow to shadow in the first place, though I'm sure she'd be appalled if she knew.

Personally, I was grateful because it meant I could indulge my obsession with Jahrdran Vilnik, slinking from shadow to shadow until I was close enough to observe him.

Never mind that he always seemed to know when I was near and would almost immediately explode into his beast form as a result.

My fascination might never have fully developed if I hadn't learned to shadow-hop and I *definitely* wouldn't have landed in my current predicament if it weren't for Professor Dewar teaching me how to pull things into the shadows with me.

She insisted Shadow could help me control my shadow monster and that I only needed to work on forging an unbreakable bond with her.

I kind of thought we already *had* an unbreakable bond, and the image Shadow sent of her wrapped around my neck, accompanied by the sound of her rumbling purr and an emphatic, *We are,* let me know she agreed, but there was no convincing Professor Dewar.

We had to prove it.

Which, as it turned out, wasn't exactly simple.

"I know you can join Kasi anytime you want, Shadow," Professor Dewar said in her kindest, most patient voice, "but you need to wait for Kasi to call you into the shadows. One day, she might be in trouble and she will need to know how to yank you from wherever you are to wherever she is."

She doesn't need to yank me, Shadow said, annoyance in her voice. About a month ago, she'd started communicating in entire sentences and was really getting good at expressing herself.

Good enough I found myself perpetually grateful that only I could hear her.

She glared at Professor Dewar, then whirled toward me. *I'll know when you're in danger, Kasi-Mew, and not because I'm your familiar.*

She'd started calling me Kasi-Mew about the same time she started sending me words and phrases. It was such a cute rendition of Kasima, that every time she said it, my heart melted a little.

Everyone else, Shadow called by their initials, if she bothered to say their names at all. For a long time, Professor Dewar was simply cat-hat and her cat, Verity, was hat-cat, which got rather confusing.

Finally, about a week ago, Professor Dewar graduated to PD, which unfortunately was also confusing, since Shadow already called Professor Dunlop PD.

Verity was still hat-cat.

Tell PD I'm not your familiar, Kasi-Mew.

I sighed. *I already did, Shadow. Many times. She doesn't listen to me.* Much to my surprise, I'd become quite adept at communicating back to Shadow. We now had entire conversations in our heads.

For the first time in my life, I was no longer all alone because Shadow was always one thought away.

"Kasi." Professor Dewar raised an eyebrow, clearly expecting me to perform miracles, an expectation I found to be rather unrealistic.

I don't want to be yanked, Kasi-Mew. Shadow sounded nervous.

Don't worry, I promised her. *I'd never yank you anywhere.*

Shadow looped my legs in a very cat-like pattern.

Even though she was made of shadows and wasn't a physical presence at all, I swear I could feel her entire body rubbing against my legs.

"That doesn't sound very comfortable for Shadow," I said to Professor Dewar.

She let out a huff of exasperation. "Shadow, come sit beside me, right now."

Shadow gave her a sulky look, but slowly slinked over to where Professor Dewar was waiting.

"The thing is, Professor, I'm not sure

Shadow's going to enjoy being yanked around. Besides, I respect her too much. I'd rather just ask."

"Yank her to you, Ms. Smith. Now!"

That was the thing about Professor Dewar. She seemed so kind and gentle at first, almost like the grandmother you'd always wanted but never had, then she turned into this stern drillmaster who expected you to perform, no matter what.

But I wasn't about to be bullied into hurting my Shadow.

So I yanked other things into the shadows with me instead.

My copy of *A Comprehensive Guide to Familiars*, the textbook Professor Dewar constantly referred to in her lessons with me, despite Shadow Cats not being listed anywhere in it. (*An annoying oversight,* Shadow had growled the first time we looked through the book. *If PD's going to insist on calling me a familiar, I should be in the very first chapter!*)

The pan of brownies Professor Dewar baked as a reward for meeting her expectations (of course, I ate one before sliding it back out of the shadows).

Professor Dewar simply gave me an admonishing look, then said, "Again."

So I snatched the ugly crocheted hat sitting on Verity's head.

Today's hat was pink and blue and in the shape of a traditional witch's hat, which seemed a bit obvious, but Professor Dewar loved crocheting gifts for her familiar, and as for Verity, well, she adored her hats, every single ugly one of them.

Which meant that stealing her hat was the best way to bring today's particular lesson to an end.

Verity went mad, yowling and attacking shadows everywhere, accomplishing nothing, of course.

I finally tossed the hat out of the shadows toward Verity.

I had the best of intentions, so it wasn't my fault Shadow chose that moment to move between Verity and me, thus causing the hat to land on *her* head, rather than Verity's.

Everyone froze for a solid minute, then Verity exploded into movement, leaping for Shadow's head.

Shadow lunged to the side and they were off, tearing around the garden, playing a crazy cat version of keep away.

Professor Dewar sighed. "Very well, Miss Smith. I suppose we're done for the day."

"Thank you, Professor. See you next week!"

I whistled for Shadow, who whirled and tossed her head, sending the hat spinning through the air.

Verity lunged and caught it in her mouth, landed and flopped over onto the ground, where she proceeded to wrestle the hat into submission.

"No, no, Verity, don't chew on those threads. No, no, give it here now." The sounds of Professor Dewar's crooning followed us back into the shadows that led us into the castle and eventually up to our suite on the fifth floor.

CHAPTER THREE

I HAD THE same roommate this year as last—Jasmine—and we shared a suite with two other women, Mikaela and Leslie, not that we ever saw Leslie.

She had a boyfriend down on the second floor and spent most of her time with him.

Mikaela said she rarely even spent the night in their room, which theoretically was against the rules, but none of us were going to report her.

Anyway, we'd moved down a floor over the summer and were now on the fifth floor. Rumor had it, when we reached Level 2 our fourth year, we'd have actual living quarters in our suites.

For now, we simply had two dorm-style rooms with a bathroom in between.

I wasn't sure I believed the rumor. It was tempting to find out, but sliding uninvited into the shadows of someone's private quarters was a great way to get caught in a magical castle full of monsters, so I'd resisted the temptation so far.

Even though I'd managed to discover the location of a certain beast's room and was *definitely* tempted.

Though that seemed a bit extreme

when I *could* choose to stop being such a coward and *stop hiding* every time he scented me and went hunting.

Unfortunately, I couldn't seem to help myself.

Instinct had me hiding every single time, simply because I knew if he found me, my life would never be the same, and what I couldn't predict was whether that would be a good thing or not.

What if he was hunting me because he recognized the scent of a shadow monster and wanted to exterminate me like all the others of my kind?

There was another option, of course.

We'd all heard about fated mates and I wasn't on board with that whole business.

And so, I avoided Jahrdran for that

reason as well.

Because I was just twenty-one when I first caught sight of him a year before and though I was now twenty-two, almost twenty-three, that still seemed entirely too young to have to deal with an overly possessive fated mate.

I *almost* hoped he was hunting to kill me instead.

Either way, I was avoiding the entire situation by hiding in the shadows whenever I sensed him nearby.

I was thinking about Jahrdran— something I did on the regular—as I approached our suite on the fifth floor, Shadow at my side.

I was reaching for the doorknob when Shadow shoved in front of me and snarled at the door.

PEPPER MCGRAW

Not again.

What's wrong, Shadow?

Wrong scent.

Great. Jasmine probably had company again.

Well, we don't have to socialize. We'll just sneak in.

Like usual.

I glanced around to be sure no one was nearby, then let my monster out, just a little, enough so that we could become mist and shadow, capable of sliding under the door.

Once inside the room, I slid from the shadows by the door to those in the closet, Shadow at my side.

Yes, I know it's a cliche—a monster in the closet—but frankly, it's a cliche because it works. For shadow monsters anyway.

Closets were full of shadows, which made them the perfect hiding spot for me, and also provided a space from which I could peek into my dorm room and take stock.

Jasmine and Mikaela were sprawled across the two beds, chatting.

Okay, that was unexpected.

Shadow was used to Mikaela visiting and never snarled when she was around, but right now was pacing inside the closet, tail swishing back and forth.

It's just Mikaela, Shadow.

Not Mikaela-scent. Other-scent.

Maybe they already left.

Shadow let out a low, rumbling growl, which was somewhat concerning.

I peeked out into the room again, but

nope.

Still just the two of them—Jasmine sprawled across her bed and Mikaela across mine.

I suppose some people might be annoyed at Mikaela for hanging out on their bed, but the truth was I never slept there.

I much preferred the shadows beneath it.

Shadows, I now realized, that were *not* empty the way they should be.

How annoying that I hadn't noticed until now.

Time to roust the intruder, Shadow.

Finally!

I slid from the shadow in the closet to one just outside it and slowly eased around the room, sliding from one shadow to the next until I reached the one at the end of the bed.

I immediately sensed that the person hiding there wasn't truly using the shadows to hide so much as they were simply using the bed.

So, not a shadow monster like me.

Now, I know what you're thinking, but it wasn't Jahrdran.

Truthfully, if it had been him, Shadow would probably have been under there with him, rubbing against him by now.

For some unknown reason, she was as obsessed with him as I was.

It wasn't Jahrdran though.

Just some other, unknown monster.

Not a very bright one, of course, since he apparently thought it was a good idea to climb under the bed of a fellow monster.

Shadow hissed again and looked up at me, as if to demand what I was going to do about this interloper.

I smirked. *On three. One. Two. Three!*

I slammed my boot against the bed frame at the same moment Shadow flung herself beneath it, exploding into multiple shadow-cats that hissed and yowled and swiped with claws.

The entire bed shook as the monster beneath it let out a high-pitched squeal and started flailing about.

At the same time, Mikaela scrambled to her feet with a gasp. "What was that?" She stared down at the bed beneath her as if she could see through the mattress to what lay beneath.

Well, for all I knew, maybe she could.

I slid back into the shadows of the closet and watched as Jasmine, who was still sprawled across her own bed, slid to the edge, leaned over it and peeked under mine.

"Vip! What are you doing?" she snarled. "Get out from under there right now!"

The monster—Vip, apparently—slid free from the bed, one hand held to his forehead, which was looking a bit red, probably from hitting his head on the bed frame, the other held to what looked to be a bleeding scratch on his arm.

Interesting.

Shadow slid from beneath the bed as well and leapt across the room, sliding into the closet to join me.

Did you actually manage to scratch him?

He was Shadow-Prey, she said smugly.

"Hey, ladies." Vip gave a smile that he probably thought was charming. "I'm just your friendly, neighborhood, monster under the bed."

"You idiot!" Jasmine exclaimed. "Go find a human's bed to crawl under. The beds of other monsters are off-limits."

"Yeah, but I heard this one *belongs* to a human."

"What are you talking about?" Mikaela snapped.

"Oh, come on. Surely you've heard the rumors."

"What rumors?" Jasmine asked.

"About your roommate. No one has a

clue what she is. She never uses any magic or powers that any of us can see *and* even though she never seems to be in class, the professors never mark her absent. Don't you think it's strange?"

"Maybe that's her power," Mikaela said.

"Yeah," Jasmine said. "Maybe she can convince people she's there when she's not."

"Or maybe she can turn invisible," Mikaela said.

"Or *maybe* she's human," Vip said.

"Or *maybe* you're just not that observant," Jasmine snapped. "Now get out and don't go crawling under my—or my roommate's—bed again."

He sighed. "Fine. But it seems a waste of a perfectly good monster-hangout spot." He headed for the door, then paused right outside the closet. He glanced into the shadowed interior, looking straight through me, then glanced back at my roommate. "What about the—"

"Out!" Jasmine exclaimed. "And don't be sneaking into our room ever again. Next time, I'll report you to the Headmistress."

With another huge sigh, he left.

"Jeez," Mikaela said. "He's lucky I didn't set the bed on fire when he startled me like that."

Jasmine chuckled. "No kidding!" She raised her voice. "Okay, Kasi. It's all clear!"

I froze in the act of sliding from a shadow inside the closet to one outside it.

I sort of hovered there, spread a little thin between the two shadows, and waited.

Jasmine was staring at the closet expectantly.

Now what should I do? This had never happened before.

I glanced down at Shadow, hoping for some advice, but she wasn't there.

Instead, I found her blinking out at me from the shadows beneath the bed.

Seriously? I demanded.

A soft, purring chuckle was her only response.

Traitor. Restraining the groan I wanted to release, I let go of my monster.

The mist and smoke retreated back into the closet and I slowly settled back into my physical form. I then dragged in a deep breath and slipped from the closet into our room.

Mikaela looked startled, but Jasmine just smiled.

I cleared my throat. "Hey. You knew I was here?"

Jasmine shrugged. "At first, I thought *you* were the one under the bed. Once I realized Vip was hanging out under there, I figured you had to be in the closet. You don't have to hide, you know. You're perfectly safe here."

I glanced at Mikaela, who was nodding in agreement. "Yeah. Perfectly safe. And don't mind Vip. He's a harmless idiot."

I nodded, then shrugged. "I like sleeping under the bed."

"A lot of monsters do," Jasmine said.

"Have a seat." Mikaela slid over and patted the bed.

I gingerly perched on the edge and eyed the two of them. "Do you always know when I'm around?"

"Not always," Jasmine said. "But at night, yeah. I knew you were still coming back to the room to sleep. I just wasn't sure if you were in the bed or under it or even just hanging out in the closet. I can't really see you, but I do sense you sometimes."

"What about you?" I asked Mikaela.

"Not a clue," she said cheerfully. "When Jasmine said your name, that's the first time I realized you were here."

"I hadn't been here long," I said, wanting to assure her I hadn't been listening to their conversation, even though technically, I'd overheard many over the past year. "Just long enough to discover *Vip* under the bed."

"He's an idiot," Jasmine repeated.

I nodded, then motioned toward the shadows beneath the bed. "I'm gonna go—"

"Sure," Jasmine said. "Good to see you."

"Yeah. You too."

I held onto my monster as I slid beneath the bed, not letting even a tiny tendril of mist escape until I was deep in the dark and neither one could see me as I relaxed into the shadowed depths beneath my bed.

The moment I was settled, Shadow leapt onto me, stretching out so that her head was just beneath my chin and her paws fell on either side of me.

Once again, even though I *knew* she was nothing more than smoke and mist, I swear I could feel the weight of her pressing into me, reminding me that I was no longer alone.

As I lay there, listening to Shadow's rumbling purr, I thought about everything I'd just learned.

First, there were rumors about me.

Second, my roommate actually knew when I was around.

And third, she and Mikaela had been nice.

An unexpected development.

Not that they'd ever been mean to me before. I mean, we had met on several occasions before, especially the previous year, before I'd learned how to travel from shadow to shadow.

Jasmine had seen me sliding out from under the bed in the mornings plenty of times and we'd developed a routine where we'd greet each other, then go our separate ways.

This year, though, I'd been working hard at keeping everyone from catching even a single glimpse of me.

Except the professors, of course.

I'd become quite adept at letting them know I was in the room, even if they couldn't see me.

Usually that involved sending them a text with my location pinned upon it.

If they pissed me off, that location would be me lurking directly behind them in the shadows.

MONSTER'S REWARD

The result was always funny, though I also always paid for it in our private lessons. More homework. Harder tasks. Greater expectations. Longer drills.

Still it was worth it, especially since I enjoyed toying with people.

Which made me wonder.

Was Jahrdran toying with me the way I toyed with our professors? The way predators toyed with their prey?

That's when it happened.

I fell asleep thinking about Jahrdran and woke in his arms.

CHAPTER FOUR

DURING THOSE LESSONS with Professor Dewar, I never did get around to yanking Shadow into the shadows with me.

Instead, I continued doing what I always did—I reached out to her and asked politely.

Of course, she always joined me immediately.

Every single time.

MONSTER'S REWARD

Still, Professor Dewar wasn't impressed.

She wanted proof that I could fetch on demand or in crisis mode and she wasn't at all appeased by the fact that I could drag any number of non-living things into the shadows with me.

She wanted proof that I could pull a living creature into the shadows without killing it.

Well, I wasn't about to practice on Shadow.

Apparently, though, my sleeping brain had no issues with practicing on Jahrdran Vilnik.

I woke in a fever.

It was so hot beneath the bed, I thought perhaps Mikaela had set it on fire, after all.

PEPPER MCGRAW

Shadow was stretched out along my back, a new position for her, and my front was nestled against a soft, furry pillow.

It took me another beat to realize arms were banded around me in a tight, possessive hug.

Shadow chose that moment to peel away from my back and slink away.

My eyes flew open and I tilted my head up to look into the eyes of the beast who held me.

"There you are," he rumbled, his blue eyes flaring bright. "I've searched this entire castle for you over and over again, mate. Why have you been hiding from me?"

"Why have you been hunting me?" I countered.

"Mate," he rumbled. "I hunt for mate. You are mine."

I wanted to protest, but seriously, how could I? This man-beast was sending me up in flames and it wasn't because of the temperature beneath the bed.

No. It was because he was seriously hot—in *both* forms.

I'd only ever seen him up close in his beast form and I found the sight incredibly sexy every time—the intense look on his furry face, the way his eyes blazed in determination, the bunch in the muscles of his thighs as he loped down the corridors, scenting and hunting me.

As for his human form, I'd only rarely caught a glimpse of it, since he almost always beasted out the second I saw him.

As a result, I really had no idea what he looked like, other than that his hair was the same color as his beast's—a deep, unrelenting black—and he retained his adorable, pointed, furry ears in his human form.

Given the shadows beneath the bed, I still couldn't see his human form clearly, but I could definitely feel it.

And what I felt was all hard muscle.

He wasn't as furry in this form, but also wasn't hairless, hence the soft pillow I'd woken against, a pillow that turned out to be his rather furry, sexy chest.

His eyes were as bright in human form as they were in beast form—an incredible, blazing shade of blue that matched the streaks in my hair that had begun to appear the day I saw him for the first time. One tiny strand of hair that had multiplied through the years as if it had a life of its own.

Shadow liked to play with those streaks, waking me each morning by batting at them, claws scraping at my scalp, purrs rumbling in her throat.

The moment my eyes would open, she would send an image of Jahrdran.

Like I said, she was as fascinated with him as I was, and was always pestering me to go find him.

Now he'd found me.

Or, more likely, my monster had dragged him to me.

I glanced around.

I was still under my bed, though there was less room with a beast at my side. "How'd you get down here anyway?"

He shrugged. "Followed the Shadow Cat."

I gasped. "Shadow? You saw her?"

"I see her all the time, but she always disappears when I go to follow. This time, when she disappeared, somehow she took me with her."

Interesting.

No one ever saw Shadow unless she wanted them to because it meant leaving the shadows, when like me, she was much more comfortable staying inside them.

She was also quite protective of me and my secret.

MONSTER'S REWARD

Since Shadow had deliberately shown herself to Jahrdran, and apparently more than once if he was to be believed, she must trust him not to harm me should he learn what I was.

This made me wonder how that trust had developed and whether she'd been going to Jahrdran each night when she left me.

Though she and I usually fell asleep together beneath the bed, she always left at some point because she was never there when I rolled over in the middle of the night.

I'd always wondered where she went and now imagined her seeking out Jahrdran.

Whether that was true or not, though, I never woke alone.

Shadow told me once that my mind would always reach out to hers when I began to wake and that was how she knew to come to me.

Now I had to wonder.

Had I reached for him as well?

"Mate," he rumbled, then rolled us so that he settled over me, his weight pressing me into the floor.

I caught my breath, eyes widening, at the feel of his huge cock nudging against my core.

He fisted his hand in my hair, dragged my head back so that my eyes were caught in his, then demanded, "Tell me your name, mate."

"Kasima," I managed to say. "I mean Kasi."

"Kasima," he rumbled, the word

sounding exotic as it tumbled from his mouth. "Kasima, my mate."

I shook my head. "I don't think—"

He lowered his head and captured my lips with his and then I wasn't thinking at all.

Every thought I had was blasted away in the searing heat of his kiss.

My heart pounded as I helplessly kissed him back.

I raked my fingers down his back, clutching, trying to get closer.

I hooked my legs around his hips and ground upward, desperate for something more.

He lifted, but I followed him, holding on as he ripped a claw down the back of my nightshirt, tearing it in two.

Then we were skin to skin.

He rubbed his chest against mine, causing the nipples to tighten.

I whimpered and clutched him closer. "Please." My head fell back. "Jahrdran."

He growled and shoved his hips forward, dragging his cock along my core, making it throb and ache.

He did it again and again until I was crying out, in both panic and ecstasy as I tumbled faster toward some unknown cliff.

"Say it again," he growled in my ear as he surged forward once more, the thin barrier of my panties proving no match for his beast.

The seam tore and then he was right there, every glorious inch of him pressing forward, stretching me to the point of pain.

MONSTER'S REWARD

"My name," he growled in my ear. "Say it again."

"Jahrdran," I gasped. "Oh, shit, Jahrdran." I wanted to say no more, it's too much, no more, but the truth was it was just right, just enough, that tiny bite of pain that edged me closer and closer to ecstasy.

And still he pressed deeper, then deeper still.

By all the saints, *how big was he?*

Finally, he bottomed out deep inside me and we both hung there, frozen on a precipice, gasping for breath.

"Again," he muttered.

This time I didn't hesitate. "Jahrdran."

He pulled back and thrust deep.

"Jahrdran, please, oh, fuck, fuck,

fuck, Jahrdran!" The last was a screech that had to hurt his ears as he powered into me over and over again, the exquisite agony of his claiming like nothing I'd ever felt before.

He pulled back and plowed forward once more, then froze there, face buried in my neck. "Mate," he grunted.

Oh, fuck.

The world shattered in brilliant shards of light as my core rippled around his cock again and again, aftershocks burning through us both, making him grunt and me cry out.

Silence fell and we lay there in each other's arms, gasping for breath, surrounded by the scent of our mating.

It was several moments longer before I realized his fangs were buried in my neck *and* his cock was knotted inside me.

Oh, *fuck.*

I knew what that meant.

My heart thundered as I tried to catch my breath, tried to decide what to do, what to say, but unable to gather any thoughts together as aftershocks continued to ripple through me, making me clench around him and causing him to jerk and groan above me.

Finally, the aftershocks tapered off and the knot loosened, easing the pressure inside.

His cock though—it was still so huge inside me and it showed no sign of deflating anytime soon.

I shifted restlessly, a compulsive movement which somehow made his massive cock feel larger still, something which should have been impossible given how it still filled me to overflowing despite having just erupted inside me.

It was that thought, that visceral memory combined with the feel of his cock still pressing against my insides that caused a massive aftershock to shudder through me.

My core clenched down and rippled around him once more.

He grunted in reaction, then pulled back until just the tip was lodged inside me, before plunging deep.

I was so wet this time, he bottomed out in an instant, before pulling back again.

Surging forward, then back, his cock scraped every nerve along the way, making me clutch at his arms, his back, and writhe beneath him, begging, begging for relief.

The hours passed, there in the shadows, him grunting and growling, me whimpering and gasping, both of us lost in each other until it seemed the entire world had disappeared.

It was only a desperate need for sustenance a couple days later that finally had us crawling from beneath the bed, only to encounter Jasmine's startled, then knowing, look.

"Wow," she said. "I had no idea you were down there." She eyed Jahrdran, who had shifted into his beast form before sliding from beneath the bed. "And I can't imagine how *you* fit, but then this place is full of mysteries, isn't it?"

That was the moment I truly understood the nature of the shadows that hid me within them.

They might be connected to the shadows of this world, but they could not possibly *be* of this world.

Instead, they must belong elsewhere so that when I went hiding within them, I disappeared from this world into that elsewhere one of shadow, where my only connection to this one became the window formed where the shadows of one world connected to the other.

This had to be how Jahrdran had fit beneath the bed with me, even though logically speaking, he should never have managed to get his human shoulders under there, let alone his entire beast form.

It was how we could spend days making love without a single scent or sound reaching the room where Jasmine slept.

And now, knowing how those shadows worked, how they sheltered me and reached for me in moments of danger or uncertainty, how they enveloped me and shielded me from the real world, pulling me into a shadow world no one else could access, I understood how I'd managed to call Jahrdran to me.

Because Jahrdran had to be my fated mate.

It was the only reasonable explanation for why the shadows hadn't ejected Jahrdran the moment I called him to me.

After all, he wasn't a shadow monster himself, so should never have been able to move into that elsewhere world of shadows with me, let alone stay there for so long.

However, as my mate, it was entirely possible he had an open invitation to join me in the shadows.

And now that our mating was official, I had to consider the very real possibility that Jahrdran Vilnik might now have full access to my shadow realm.

CHAPTER FIVE

JAHRDRAN WAS AS possessive a bastard as I assumed he would be.

Somehow, though, I liked it.

He followed me everywhere, growling at anyone who looked at me longer than five seconds.

Male or female, young or old, it didn't matter.

To him, I was the most desirable person in all the realms, so he couldn't imagine that I wasn't also desirable to every other person I met.

We had a few whispered, heated conversations that first day after our mating when he tried to go with me to my Year 2 classes instead of attending his own Year 3 ones.

It was only my promise to stay in the shadows so no one could see me (something I always did anyway) that finally convinced him to walk away.

But not before grabbing me behind the neck, yanking me into his arms and kissing me breathless.

For the next several weeks, every free minute I had was consumed by Jahrdran. He walked me to and from class, even when it meant he would be late to his own classes or have to leave them early.

Of course, every greeting and farewell began and ended with a blazing, hot kiss deep in the shadows of whatever classroom he'd walked me into or was about to lead me out of.

The most shocking turn of events was that I discovered I loved having a fated mate. I loved *being* the fated mate of Jahrdran.

In fact, I enjoyed being his mate so much that for a while I forgot my quest, the one that had me searching for clues to my origins for the past year.

I even forgot the danger inherent in someone discovering my secrets.

I simply reveled in being the mate of my beloved beast.

Until the day everything changed.

MONSTER'S REWARD

We'd both returned to my room because for the next hour, Jasmine would be in her Culinary Delights Cooking class, and then would hang out with her friends, taste-testing everything they'd cooked that day.

We'd just finished an intense bout of lovemaking, on *top* of the bed this time, and I was nestled between Jahrdran's legs, my back against his chest, his arms wrapped around me.

One large hand was gently stroking me from my neck down, long, slow strokes of his hand that lit fires everywhere, while the other hand was playing with my blue streaks.

He loved those blue streaks even more than Shadow did and had informed me they were a physical reminder to everyone that I belonged to him.

I'd just rolled my eyes at him. "Maybe your eyes are a sign that *you* belong to *me.*"

Of course, beast that he was, he'd looked pleased at the thought, then had rumbled quietly, "Probably it means we belong to each other. Mates for life."

I grinned at the memory.

"Are you ever going to tell me what type of supernatural you are?" Jahrdran's voice interrupted my reverie.

I stiffened, uncertainty filling me.

I wanted to tell him, but what if the professors were right? What if sharing my secrets meant losing him?

What if it made us enemies?

"Hey," Jahrdran murmured. "We're mates. Nothing you can say will ever change that."

I wanted to believe him.

I *did.*

But I was afraid.

"They told me not to say anything," I muttered.

"What? Who?"

"Headmistress Blackthorn. Professor Dunlop. The other professors. Mr. Brecken."

"The *librarian?*" Jahrdran asked incredulously.

I shrugged. "I've been researching in the libraries, looking for more information about my kind and our history. He figured out what I was and admonished me not to tell anyone. Not *anyone.*"

"Huh. That's weird. I can't imagine

any supernatural that would cause so much—" He broke off and his arms tightened around me compulsively.

"Jahrdran?"

"Shadow," he breathed.

"What?"

"I knew she was a shadow cat, but I just figured she was one of the magical creatures wandering the castle grounds. After all, the shadow cats are almost gone from this world. They all faded when their Monsters died."

Silence fell as he processed.

I didn't speak, afraid to even admit he was on the right track.

He suddenly lunged upward with me in his arms.

He turned and set me back on the bed, grabbed his jeans and began to dress, agitation in every movement.

Dread tightened my throat.

I leaned over, grabbed my t-shirt off the floor and quickly pulled it over my head.

I wanted to approach Jahrdran, touch him, remind him that I was still me, but he was standing, hands on hips, staring down at the floor and I was frozen in fear.

Afraid of what he was about to say.

Finally, with a deep breath, he turned to face me. "She's not just some random creature you happened to make friends with, is she? Shadow's your familiar." He said it almost accusingly.

I shook my head. I didn't know what I was saying no to—that she wasn't my familiar, that she wasn't a familiar at all, that he needed to stop before everything fell apart.

But I could see it on his face.

He already knew. He'd already figured everything out.

"That's your secret, isn't it, Kasima? You're a shadow monster."

I wanted to deny it.

Because despite his claim that my secrets didn't matter, that our mating was solid, I could sense that *everything* was about to change.

"Just say it," he growled.

"Yes. I'm a shadow monster."

He shuddered, then gave me a look of such horror, I actually felt my heart crack in two.

"You said nothing would change," I whispered. "You said we were mates forever and nothing would change that."

"You should have told me," he said.

"When? When, Jahrdran? When would have been the right time for you to discover your mate is a shadow monster?"

"When we first met," he growled. "Immediately."

"You mated me the minute we met! Was I supposed to just blurt it out in the middle of our mating?" My heart pounded in my chest and I could barely catch my breath. "Would it really have made a difference?"

What I really wanted to know was whether it would have stopped him from mating me, but I was afraid to ask.

"Of course, it would have. You're a shadow monster and I'm—"

"What? You're what?"

He glared at me. "How can you ask me that? How can you not know what you've done?"

I shook my head. "I'm in the dark here, Jahrdran. I never knew about the supernatural world until right before arriving here. I've lived in the human world my entire life. The professors tell me nothing, just what I am and that I have to keep it a secret. They don't even tell me why."

"Because once upon a time, a shadow monster wreaked hell upon the earth, trapping humans and supernaturals alike within the shadow realm. No matter how hard the other shadow monsters worked to save those trapped there, millions died. *Millions.*"

I blanched. Here were the answers I'd been seeking all this time and my mate had known them all along.

How was it that he could know my entire history, yet the professors at the Academy dictated that I could not?

"Do you know what it's like for someone not of the shadow realm to be trapped there? To die there?"

I shook my head mutely.

"The shadows wrap around them, fill them up, then consume them from the inside out. It's a terribly slow death. It takes time for the darkness to fully digest them. And those who were saved from death weren't actually saved at all because they were never the same. They came back different, full of darkness that ate them from the inside out. They turned into serial killers and worse until it was accepted that anyone trapped in the shadow realm had to stay there.

"So then, instead of sending shadow monsters into the shadows to rescue those trapped, they became executioners, sent to end their suffering."

"I don't understand," I said quietly. "How does this story end with the *shadow monsters* being hunted and executed? They were just trying to help, right?"

"Yes, after one of them caused the problem in the first place."

"So the entire race was punished?"

"You have to understand, Kasi. No one knew which shadow monster it was who went rogue. It could have been any of them, or even many of them. And the worst part was that once it got out that the shadow realm was twisting its victims into something dark, those same rogue monsters were setting them free.

"Imagine it. Hordes of darkened creatures, serial killers all of them, being pulled into the other realms, causing death and destruction everywhere. In the end, it was decided that every single shadow monster presented a clear and present danger to all of civilization, and so, the entire race was put under a death order."

"So one shadow monster—or several," I amended at the look on his face, "did truly horrific things and my entire race gets exterminated for it?"

He sighed. "I know it sounds harsh,

but trust me, it was necessary."

The problem was I didn't trust him.

Not anymore.

Not since he'd started looking at me as if *I* were that long-ago monster wreaking havoc through the realms.

"Look, there are shadows in every universe, which meant the shadow monsters and their familiars had access to everyone, everywhere, at any time. A decision had to be made."

"How do you know all this?"

He stared at her. "I'm a Varulvka."

"I know that. You told me that already. What does that have to do with anything?"

"The Varulvka are a race of elite hunters. When the shadow monsters were condemned, we were the ones sent out to enact justice."

I leapt to my feet. "Justice? Since when is genocide justice?"

"When it saves entire civilizations—" he began.

"Genocide?" I repeated incredulously. "You would have been killing children. *Babies.*"

"Not me," he said quickly. "This was hundreds of years before I was born."

"So your ancestors destroyed mine. Is that what you're telling me?"

He nodded.

"Okay, fine, but all of this happened way before either of us was ever born," I started speaking faster, trying to get my thoughts out as quickly as possible, as if I could somehow stave off what I sensed was coming. "I'm not going to go trapping anyone in the shadow realm and you're not an executioner like your ancestors were. So we'll be fine. We'll just keep my secret, I won't tell anyone else and—"

"We're not *fine*, Kasi," he snarled.

I froze.

"I've sworn an oath. Do you understand? An *oath*. To protect the realms from any and all dangers and *you* are a danger. *Every* shadow monster is a danger. It's *why* they were eliminated from all the realms."

"But I—"

"*No*, Kasi. Don't you understand what I'm expected to *do* now that I know what you are? My oath would have me executing you without any hesitation whatsoever. I've *already* broken that oath by not executing the shadow cat the minute I saw her, but I figured she couldn't cause any harm here, without a Monster controlling her." He glared at Kasi, accusation in his gaze.

"I don't control Shadow! I don't know how, and even if I did, I wouldn't want to." My heart was pounding so hard, I could barely get out my next question. "So, what? You're going to assassinate your mate? Is that the plan now?"

He shook his head. "I don't know, Kasi. Just don't—just stay away from me and I'll stay away from you and I'll try to forget we ever had this conversation." He walked toward the door.

"So that's it?" To my fury, my voice cracked a little. "You're just going to walk away? From us?"

He froze, his hand on the door. "I don't know what you want me to say, Kasi." He spoke facing the door, refusing to look back at me, refusing to give me even a moment more of his regard. "I took an oath, an oath that would have me killing you right now. But I can't do it. You're my mate, so I can't. But that's all I can give you, Kasi. A stay of execution. That's all.

"So keep your head down, don't show your monster to anyone and don't *ever* pull someone into the shadows like you did me when we first mated. All this time I thought it was Shadow pulling you and me into the shadows, but it was *you* all along.

"Never again, Kasi. Do you understand? You do it again and I won't have a choice. I *will* kill you if I have to."

He opened the door and walked away.

CHAPTER SIX

I'VE NEVER BEEN so angry in my entire life. I fed the anger because as long as I did that, I could stave off the devastation boiling beneath it.

So, anger it was.

I just couldn't decide who I was angrier with.

Jahrdran for rejecting me or my professors for not giving me critical information I *needed* in order to avoid this entire fiasco.

If they had just *told* me my own history, I would have known to avoid Jahrdran at all costs and would never have mated with him.

Probably.

At the very least, I wouldn't have allowed my obsession to get so out of control that I was constantly lurking in the shadows, watching him.

And without me obsessively stalking him, I probably wouldn't have pulled him into the shadows with me in the first place.

Which meant he may never have claimed me as his mate, then later, rejected me, leaving me in this impossible situation.

A situation I had no idea how to fix.

PEPPER MCGRAW

Was there any way to fix it?

And more importantly, did I even want to?

The pain I felt at his rejection was unlike anything I'd ever felt before. The loneliness that had diminished when I found Shadow and that had completely disappeared in the past few weeks since mating with Jahrdran was back with a vengeance and it was way worse than before.

Now I knew what I was missing.

Now I knew what it felt like to be cherished, to be the mate of someone who would do anything for you.

And now I knew what it felt like to be rejected by that same mate for something that wasn't even your fault, for something completely out of your control, for something as simple and immutable as your genetic makeup.

Even if I could fix things, somehow convince Jahrdran to give us a chance, I don't know that I could ever forgive him *or* trust him again.

I was still lying on my bed, where I'd collapsed after Jahrdran left, curled into a ball with Shadow wrapped around me, when Jasmine and Mikaela came into the room, laughing.

The minute they caught sight of me, they both froze and stared.

"Oh, Kasi," Jasmine gasped. "What happened?"

"What are you talking about?" I asked, my voice sounding completely foreign to my ears, lifeless and lost.

"You're *crying*," Mikaela exclaimed.

I lifted a hand to my cheek and realized she was right.

Tears were slowly trickling down my face in an outward display of the heartache I was now experiencing.

I couldn't understand it.

How had he become so important to me in such a short amount of time?

How could losing him send me spiraling like this?

"Are you okay?" Jasmine sat beside me on the bed.

"Should I get Jahrdran?" Mikaela asked.

"No!" I exclaimed hoarsely, scrambling to a sitting position.

Shadow crept around me, sliding into my lap and stretching upward, so that somehow her entire body was connected to my front, her face buried in my neck, her purr rumbling through me, a reminder that even though my heart was breaking, I was still not alone.

"No," I said again. "He–he–" I broke off as a new spate of tears poured down my face.

"Oh no," Jasmine said softly. "What happened? He's okay, right?"

The question stalled me for a moment because it made me realize they thought maybe he'd been hurt or even killed, but then wouldn't the pain of that be better than this? At least then I'd know he didn't leave me willingly.

Besides, given that we'd mated, I'd quite possibly have followed him to the next life, where we wouldn't even have to worry about the ridiculous histories of our ancestors.

"He's fine," I said bitterly.

I could see the confusion on their faces, so I added, just because I knew I'd have to tell them eventually, "He broke up with me." A ridiculously generic phrase that couldn't possibly convey the cruelty behind the act or the devastation it had caused me.

"What?" Jasmine and Mikaela gasped in unison.

"That can't be right, Kasi," Jasmine said. "The way he acted around you, I was sure you two were mates."

"Yeah," Mikaela agreed. "There's no way he'd—"

"He did," I said harshly. "He rejected me."

"I'm shocked," Jasmine said bluntly.

"Although I suppose if he met his fated mate—"

The thought of it sent fury through me. "*I'm* his fated mate," I snarled, the shadow monster in me stretching and unfurling at the thought of Jahrdran attempting to mate with *anyone* other than us. "He's mated to me!"

"Wait. You already mated?" Mikaela asked.

I nodded.

"I knew it!" Jasmine crowed, but her excitement died almost immediately as she frowned in confusion. "But then why in the world would he break up with you? It doesn't make any sense. He—"

"Jasmine." Mikaela spoke her name softly.

Jasmine glanced at Mikaela, who

shook her head silently, then carefully sat on my other side.

She drew in a deep breath, then asked quietly, "He found out what you are, didn't he?"

I froze, unable to breathe, unable to process what was happening.

Did *everyone* know my secret?

"What are you talking about, Mikaela?" Jasmine asked. "What is she?"

I breathed a little easier. So Jasmine didn't know.

Maybe Mikaela didn't either.

"She's a shadow monster."

I bit my lip, anxiety pouring through me.

Was I about to lose my only other friends at the Academy?

"What's a shadow monster?" Jasmine

asked.

"They were monsters who could take the form of shadows and then use them to travel pretty much everywhere in the known universes," Mikaela said, "maybe even the unknown ones, but then they were supposedly all executed hundreds of years ago, which makes Kasi a complete mystery."

"I've been searching the Academy library for the past two years, trying to find any reference to shadow monsters," I said, "and it's as if we never existed, so how'd you find out about us?"

Mikaela smirked. "I may have read my mother's collection of *Special Editions* over the summer."

Mikaela's mother was a high-ranking official in the witching community, which meant she had an extensive library and knew where *all* the skeletons were buried, at least the witchy ones.

"Okay, so Kasi's a shadow monster," Jasmine said, "but why would Jahrdran reject her because of it?"

"Are you sure you want to know?" I asked bitterly.

"He didn't reject her just because she's a shadow monster," Mikaela said. "He rejected her because *he's* one of the Varulvka."

"Yes," I said, "because his *oath* is more important than his mate."

"Well, it *is* an important oath," Jasmine said. "Varulvka are protectors of the realms, after all, but I still don't understand why that would force him to reject you. You're not a danger."

"According to Jahrdran, I am." I then told her the story of the rogue shadow monster and how that story had ended in genocide.

"So, let me get this straight," Jasmine said. "There used to be a lot of shadow monsters like Kasi, but then, one of them went rogue and no one could capture him or her, so the entire species was hunted and killed? Even the babies?" Jasmine sounded as horrified as I'd been when I'd learned the fate of my people.

"Pretty much," Mikaela said.

"Yep," I agreed glumly.

"Although, according to my mom," Mikaela said, "there's the remote possibility that the rogue wasn't a shadow monster at all."

"Wait, *what?*" I exclaimed. Not a single professor had mentioned this possibility.

"It's just a theory," Mikaela said, "but my mom says there's a pretty good chance it's correct."

"I don't understand," Jasmine said. "So an entire species might have been wiped out for nothing?"

"If it wasn't a shadow monster, who was dragging people into the shadows?" I demanded.

"I don't know," Mikaela said.

"Honestly, as far as I'm concerned, genocide was an overreaction, regardless of who was it was," I said. "My people were unfairly executed—most, if not all of them, innocent of any crime. So, the fact that it might not have been a shadow monster wouldn't even matter to me, except—" I stopped because I wasn't even sure I should want what I'd been about to say.

"It might make a difference for Jahrdran?" Jasmine asked gently.

I nodded. "Not that he deserves a second chance, but—"

"He's your mate," Mikaela said.

I nodded.

"So what do you want to do?" Jasmine asked.

"I need to find out the truth."

Never mind that I'd had no luck in my search so far. In a single day, in two conversations, one with my mate and one with my friends, I'd discovered more truths than I had in more than a year, and I was determined to keep that streak going.

"That's going to be awfully difficult," Mikaela said, "considering there just aren't that many reliable records from that time. Most monsters today believe the shadow monsters were a myth. I've read the majority of my mother's library and only found one reference to the shadow monsters in the entire collection."

I nodded. "I'm not surprised, considering I've done thousands of searches in the Academy library and have come up with nothing."

"Have you searched the archives room?" Jasmine asked.

I shook my head. "None of the professors will give me permission."

"But that makes no sense," Jasmine

exclaimed. "I mean, sure, we have to get special permission, and Mr. Brecken usually hovers to make sure we're not doing anything dastardly with his books, but—"

"Mr. Brecken told me the headmistress specifically forbade him from allowing me to set foot in the archives room," I said.

"But that's huge, Kasi," Mikaela said. "It means there's probably something important inside the room."

"I know, but the door is sealed and he won't even crack the door if I'm in the library. Someone comes in, asking to visit the archives and he tells them to come back later or he asks me to leave. The professors all know I can use the shadows to travel, so he's not taking a chance I might shadow-hop right into the archives."

"Well, then, we'll just have to work together to get you inside," Jasmine said.

CHAPTER SEVEN

IT WAS A terrible plan, but I had no other ideas to offer, so we went with it.

Jasmine and Mikaela led the way into the library while I shifted into my shadow form and streamed in their wake, Shadow at my side.

We slid from the shadow the library door cast across the floor to the ones that ran alongside the long shelves of books. We slipped from one shadow to the next until we reached the shadows closest to the archive room, then hovered there waiting as Jasmine and Mikaela charmed Mr. Brecken into allowing them inside.

"Now, what exactly are you researching again?" Mr. Brecken asked as he slowly made his way across the library floor, a ring of keys in his hand.

"It's for our Monsters Throughout History class," Jasmine said.

"We're researching serial killer monsters for our semester project," Mikaela said.

Mr. Brecken grimaced. "Now why would the two of you want to research such a depressing subject?"

"I'm interested in justice studies," Mikaela said, "and how the different factions of supernaturals police their own."

"And you thought to start with monsters?" he glanced at Mikaela from the corner of his eye, a skeptical look on his face.

How could he already be suspicious? Convincing him to let them inside the archive room wasn't supposed to be the hard part.

"Well, no. I've already done quite a bit of research. My mom's collection really helped me understand how justice works for witches and vampires and even some shifter societies. I'm interested in learning more, though."

"Ah. Well, I don't know what you'll find inside the Archives on justice specifically."

"Oh, I don't usually search for the word justice. Punishment is more the thing with supernaturals."

"Yes, well. You'll be careful with the collections, of course."

"Of course," Mikaela and Jasmine chorused.

With a nod, he unlocked the door with one of his keys, then carefully extracted it from the lock before starting to open the door.

The door was about half open when Jasmine exclaimed, "Oh, dear, I completely forgot."

Mr. Brecken slowly turned and faced Jasmine and Mikaela, who hovered just behind him, as if they'd been about to follow him into the room.

"Forgot what?" he asked.

PEPPER MCGRAW

He stood like a sentinel in the half-open doorway, his right arm stretching across the space, hand clutching the doorknob tight, preventing anyone from entering without his permission.

The room was completely dark behind him, which was unfortunate, for no shadows could form in darkness.

Some light from the rest of the library did filter in, though, just enough for Mr. Brecken's form to cast a shadow in the small triangle of light formed by the open door.

A bit of luck had the shadow of Mr. Brecken's arm touching both the shadow where I was sheltering and his own that stretched behind him.

I took immediate advantage, sliding from beneath the shelves in the library to the shadow of his arm and from there to where his shadow stretched across the threshold between library and archives.

"I'm supposed to bring a new recipe to Culinary Delights tomorrow," Jasmine said.

I happened to know that Jasmine already had an entire folder full of recipes waiting to be shared with her classmates.

I smirked as I made the quick leap from behind Mr. Brecken to behind the door.

If he'd been facing me, I would never have taken that risk, for without a shadow waiting for me, there was a high probability he'd have seen me, which might not have mattered were it not for the fact that Mr. Brecken knew what I was.

Like the majority of the professors at the Academy, if he saw shadow and mist, he would immediately assume it was me using my Shadow-form.

"Can't it wait?" Mikaela demanded.

"Not really. I'll be completely stressed out if I don't get it now. Mr. Brecken, do you have any cookbooks in the library?"

"We have an entire collection on the second floor." Mr. Brecken said.

"Could you show me?"

"If you want me to take you, I'll have to lock this door and Mikaela will need to wait until we return to visit the archives."

"Fine," Mikaela said, "but let's be quick, all right?

MONSTER'S REWARD

The door closed and the sound of the lock turning echoed in the silence of the archive room.

I stood frozen for a moment in the darkness, then let out a breath of relief when Shadow brushed against my legs, reminding me that I wasn't alone.

I was used to feeling the weight of Shadow, even though she had no real, physical form, but I was stunned to realize I could also feel her when in my shadow-form.

I drew my shadows in, settling back into my physical form, then leaned over and stroked Shadow up and down her sides. "Let's see what we can find out, shall we?"

I lifted a hand and whispered the first spell I had learned at the Academy.

"Luceat."

The room brightened as if the sun had suddenly risen in the sky, even though I was inside a room without windows.

The archive room was bigger than I had expected. There were aisles of shelves branching off in every direction from where I stood.

I chose one at random and walked it quickly, scanning the spines of books as I did so.

Vampyr Lore, From Blood to Grave, The Study of Blood, The Age of the Vampyr, The Fall of the Empire, Mythology and Reality: The Rise of Vampyrism. The list went on and on.

"Great," I muttered to Shadow as she paced by my side. "We found the vampire section. Not exactly what I was looking for."

I finally reached the end of the aisle and glanced to my left and then my right.

There were rows in both directions and I was overwhelmed at the enormity of the task I was facing. How was I to find what surely felt like a needle in a haystack without even the help of a librarian?

As far as I could tell, there was no technology in this room to do a word search, no old school card catalog, nothing. How was I going to find *anything* in this room?

I don't suppose you know where the shadow monster section is? I asked Shadow.

Shadows, she replied.

What does that mean?

Shadow-beast, shadow-cat, shadow-room, shadow-shelves, shadow-books, shadow-secrets.

"Sounds a bit convoluted," I said out loud, glancing around the room. *So, you're saying we should look for a shadow room?*

With shadow shelves.

Got it. And I assume the shelves will have shadow books?

With shadow secrets.

Okay, first things first. If you were a shadow room, where would you be hiding?

I don't know, Kasi-mew.

In shadows, certainly, deep and dark ones I assume. But where would that be?

I turned to the left and started walking, Shadow at my side.

To my right was the back wall of the archive room and all along it were cubicles for researchers to sit and work at, one at the end of each row of books.

As I walked, I glanced at each work station and the shadows it cast upon the wall and the floor, then down each row, at the shadows cast by the tall shelves looming high.

Though shadows were everywhere, none seemed deep enough or dark enough to hide an entire room and they certainly weren't big enough.

"Of course, the room is probably in the shadow realm, so it's not like it has to fit in any of *these* shadows, right?"

Shadow-things fit in any shadow, big

or small.

I grinned down at Shadow. *True. Problem is, I'm just not feeling it, at least not here with these shadows.*

So we walked on.

A few moments later, we reached the end of the room.

Just beyond the final work station, the back and side walls of the archive room met in a corner made up entirely of shadows so dark, even I couldn't quite see into them.

Shadows!

"Good job, my sweet shadow-kitten."

Shadow preened, then whirled and stared back the way we came. *MB coming back with Jam.*

Jam was her special name for Jasmine and Mikaela.

MONSTER'S REWARD

Hurry. I slid into the shadows waiting in the corner and at the last moment, whispered, *Finis.*

I sensed more than saw the library falling to darkness and hoped I'd been faster than Mr. Brecken and *Jam*, but there was no way to know because I was already being pulled elsewhere.

It was so dark where we stood, I almost felt as if I was suffocating. The only thing that kept me sane was the feel of Shadow pressing against my legs, reminding me once again that I wasn't alone.

She pressed harder, pushing me forward, and I yielded, stepping further into the unknown, relieved when she followed me.

With Shadow guiding me, we stepped

through where the corner should have been, through where the walls should have met in that corner, signaling the end of the archive room, and further into the unrelenting dark.

We had definitely shadow-walked into another space entirely.

Whether it was simply another room in the castle, a section of the shadow realm that was darker than I'd ever seen, or a completely different universe, I had no idea.

We moved forward, one hesitant step at a time, until the darkness pulled back just a little, revealing a small room made entirely of shadows.

They were everywhere, a smoky gray that obscured the floor I could feel beneath my feet and the walls around us.

Shadow-room!

Good job, Shadow. You found it.

A set of shelves stretched from shadow–floor to shadow–ceiling directly across from where we stood. *Shadow-shelves, Kasi-mew.*

I see that.

She led the way toward the shelves. *Shadow-books.*

Yes. You were right.

Like the room itself, the shelves didn't seem to be there entirely, for they shifted in darkness, smoky shadows that formed nebulous shelves and a wall behind them.

Everything in this room seemed to be in shadow-form, including the books that lined the shelves, all of them wavering before me.

Shadows obscured their titles at first, but then retreated just enough to reveal them when I focused my attention on their spines.

A History of Shadows, The Dangers of the Shadow Realm, Shades and Shadows, Shadow-Walking, The Age of Shadows, Caring for your Shadow-Kitten, A Shadow-Beast's Guide to the Shadow Realm, A Thousand Years of Shadow-Art, The Greatest Shadow Philosophers, An Analysis of the Treaty of Shades.

It was an extraordinary feeling, standing there, staring at so many books that validated my very existence, that proved my kind had once lived and lived well enough to have a rich history that spanned millennia.

I reached for the shadow-kitten book. The moment I touched it, the shadows retreated, giving it weight and substance.

I pulled it down and marveled at its weight.

I set it on the shadow-table that stood off to the side, then watched as the table solidified the moment the book touched it.

I turned back to the shelves, selected the two books about the shadow realm, set them on the table and then reached for the history book.

I opened it to its copyright page and was disappointed to discover it was three hundred years old.

This book, then, would not cover what had happened a couple hundred years ago when the shadow monsters were hunted and exterminated.

In fact, now that I thought about it, it was doubtful any book written by the shadow monsters themselves would cover those events as they'd have been busy fleeing for their lives at the time.

Damn. Everyone knows history is written by the victors. I settled at the table with my history book and smiled as Shadow leapt up and immediately plopped down on top of it. *We need a Shadow historian or some other shadow monster who knows their history.* I stroked a hand down Shadow's side and listened to her purr. *There had to have been survivors, right? Otherwise, I'd never have been born.*

Hiding.

I let out a sound of exasperation, annoyed because that was probably true. If there'd been any survivors at all, they'd probably gone into hiding, which begged the question:

How come I'm not in hiding with them?

Shadow had no answer for me and I was becoming more conscious of time passing every minute we remained inside the shadow room.

I'd probably already stayed too long and now risked being locked in there until someone came along and convinced Mr. Brecken to let them in the archive room.

If nothing else, I knew Mikaela and Jasmine would come back to ask for another peek if I failed to show back up in our suite, but in the meantime, they'd be worried and Shadow and I would be trapped.

I was flipping faster and faster through one of the books about the shadow realm, trying to somehow absorb the knowledge it offered by touch alone.

It wasn't working and I was running out of time.

Even knowing this, I couldn't make myself choose a single book to take with me. I wanted them all.

Shadow let out a huff, probably annoyed that I'd stopped petting her in favor of frantically skimming giant tomes, and jumped down from the table.

She began a slow stalk around the perimeter of the room while I immediately turned my attention to the history book she'd uncovered.

Just looking at the Table of Contents was enough to make me crave every single bit of knowledge between its covers.

What if I never made it back inside the archive room and this was my only chance to learn about the shadow realm and the history of shadow monsters?

Worse, what if this was my only chance to learn about shadow-cats? What if my ignorance caused her harm?

There were so many books to read in this room and I had no plan for transporting even one of them.

I hadn't even thought to bring a bag with me, probably because I knew it would be hard enough to time it right for my own escape, let alone to steal books while I was at it.

Of course, it hadn't occurred to me that I might gain access to a room Mr. Brecken probably didn't even know existed, or if he did, didn't know how to access, which meant he'd probably have no idea if I took any books out of said room in the first place.

Too bad I hadn't thought far enough ahead to plan for that eventuality.

Shadow-door, Shadow announced, standing at the end of the wall of books, staring at the corner just beyond them.

It was opposite the corner we'd entered from, which was intriguing to say the least.

Is it an actual door?

It has a knob.

Interesting. I hurried to join her and

immediately saw she was right. There *was* a door, and as one might expect in a shadow-room, it wavered and moved with the shadows around it.

Where do you think it goes, Kasimew?

I don't know, Shadow, but let's take a peek.

I don't know what I expected, but it wasn't what we found when we opened the door.

Water bowl. Shadow stepped forward and lifted a paw as if she was about to splash it in the water.

It's a toilet, Shadow. Don't play in it.

Toilet?

That was when I realized that no matter how close we'd gotten, Shadow had never accompanied me to the bathroom.

Uh, litter box?

She just looked at me. *What's a litter box?*

It's where mortal cats go to do their business.

Mortal cats have businesses?

No. Never mind. Just don't play in that water. It's not good for you. Now, come back in here and help me decide what books to take with me.

We slipped back into the shadow-room, where Shadow continued to explore and I perused book titles and added a couple more to my stack.

I now had seven books and I had no idea how I was going to get them back to my room. I'd probably have to make several trips.

MONSTER'S REWARD

Just as I was trying to decide which books to carry back first, Shadow came bounding up to me dragging a bookbag with her.

Where'd you find this? I carefully extracted the handles from her mouth.

Shadow-rack. She bounded to another corner, where if I squinted, I could just make out the shadowy form of what appeared to be a tall coat rack.

Fabulous job, Shadow. This should do nicely. The bag wasn't that big, but as I settled books inside it, I realized it was somehow enchanted because it was definitely holding more books than it should.

I worried at first because when I put the first book inside the bag, the book simply vanished, but if I reached deep, I could feel it and pull it free again.

It must be somehow connected to the shadow realm. I've got to learn how to enchant objects like this!

I was doubly determined once all seven books were packed away and, upon slinging the bag over my shoulder, I discovered it hardly weighed anything at all.

It's a miracle bag, I proclaimed to Shadow, *and you're a miracle for discovering it.*

Shadow let out a rumble of happiness, then led me back to the shadow-door.

We slipped through it into the bathroom stall and I turned to study the door as we let it close behind us.

The minute it closed, the outline

disappeared and it was as if the door had never existed at all.

I pushed on the wall, but nothing happened.

Well, this wasn't great at all. How was I to get back inside if it was all sealed off?

Shadow coiled herself around my legs, brushing against the wall.

The minute her shadows connected with the wall, the outline of the door reappeared and shadows spread across it, some coiling together to form a doorknob.

As Shadow looped around me, her shadows disconnecting from the wall, the door disappeared again.

Interesting. Step back, Shadow, I'm going to see if my shadows can call it forth.

She settled on her haunches and watched as I dissolved my right hand into shadows and reached for the wall.

The moment I touched it, the doorway began to form.

I spun to face Shadow. *This is fabulous. We'll be able to come back whenever we want, do as much research as we want and we won't have to ask Mr. Brecken for permission. Let's go read some books, shall we?*

CHAPTER EIGHT

IT TURNED OUT that Shadow and I beat Jasmine and Mikaela back to our suite by a couple hours.

I have the best roommates.

They wanted to give me as much opportunity as possible to do what research I could and also to escape the archive room, so they spent hours in that room with Mr. Brecken, asking him questions and exploring the stacks.

"We actually learned a lot," Mikaela said. "Just not about shadow monsters. They weren't mentioned in a single monster book we looked at."

"The Varulvka were though," Jasmine said.

"I took a lot of notes," Mikaela said. "Jahrdran wasn't kidding when he said they were exceptional hunters." She looked down and read from her spiral notebook, "'The Varulvka are elite hunters, only called upon when every other attempt has failed. They have a one hundred percent success rate. Whether that's accurate or simply because no one ever talks about their failures, is anyone's guess.'"

"Well, they had to have failed at some point," I said, "because I'm here and I'm only twenty-two years old."

"Your origin story is completely intriguing," Jasmine said. "So did you find anything when you were in there by yourself?"

I grinned. "I found an entire secret room, only accessible to shadow monsters and their shadow-cats." I then proceeded to tell them everything we'd discovered in that room and where it led.

"The locker room?" Jasmine exclaimed incredulously.

"Yep, straight into the larger stall at the end. We were lucky no one was in it at the time. Next time, I'll go in that way and lock the stall behind me."

"Does that mean you're going to have to swim every time you visit the shadow-room?" Jasmine asked.

"Not if I can help it," I said. "I'll wear workout clothes and if anyone sees me, I'll pretend I'm going to work out in the gym."

"So what books did you bring back?" Mikaela asked.

We spent the next several hours exploring the books I'd brought back with me and making a plan for our next steps.

Over the next several weeks, I made multiple trips to the shadow-room, bringing up more and more books for us to go through.

Jasmine and Mikaela helped me with the reading and the three of us became experts on all things shadow related.

I had a moment of misgiving in the beginning, wondering if I should be guarding Shadow-secrets from anyone not born of the shadows, but then I decided I desperately needed the help. Otherwise, it would take me ten years, bare minimum, to make it through the entire collection inside the shadow-room.

Instead, with Mikaela on my team (she was quite the speed-reader), we were making amazing progress.

We learned a *lot* about the ancient history of shadow monsters and about the shadow realm—so much so, in fact, that I found myself hesitating before stepping back into the shadows.

For a couple weeks, I became quite hesitant and I didn't like it.

So, I shifted the focus of my reading to the shadow realm itself.

Every free moment I had, I was in the

shadow-room or in my room, reading everything I could get my hands on to prepare me for anything and everything that might arise in the shadow realm.

By the time a month had passed, my wariness had fallen away again and I was becoming quite adept at leaping through the shadows.

I'd learned so much about shadow-walking that I no longer needed the shadows to connect in order to move from one to the next.

I only needed to see them now, which meant that I could stand at the top of the stairs on the fifth floor, lean over the railing to find a shadow—perhaps one directly under the second floor landing—and in an instant, could leap from the shadow currently sheltering me to the one I'd chosen by sight.

I learned so much in that first month and yet, I still failed in my goals.

I'd learned nothing about what had happened two hundred years before and I had no clues as to who the culprit really was.

Maybe it *had* been a shadow-beast and I was simply deluding myself, but I couldn't stop searching.

I had to know.

For me.

For Shadow.

For all the innocent shadow monsters killed in an effort to catch a serial killer.

Had they all died in vain?

We'd made it through about a third of the books in the shadow-room and I was truly dismayed that I was no closer to an answer to that question than when we'd begun.

I kept the book, *A History of Shadows* on my nightstand. Mikaela and Jasmine had both tried to read it, but whenever they opened it, the pages were completely blank.

I'd tried to hold the book for them, but somehow it knew and wouldn't show them a single word, even with me standing right there.

We finally had to accept that only I would be able to read it, which was terrible news for me, because quite frankly, it was so dry and boring, I kept falling asleep anytime I attempted to read it.

Who knew history could be so *boring?*

I'd suffer through it, though, if I

thought it would help, but since the copyright was a full hundred years before the time period I was interested in, I kept giving up.

Perhaps that was why it took me so long to notice.

One day, though, I had an unexpected afternoon free due to a class cancellation and I was determined to make some headway in the book.

I was startled at how heavy it was when I hauled it off the bottom shelf of my nightstand.

Am I imagining things, Shadow, or is this book quite a bit larger than it was before?

Shadow wasn't really interested in the books that much, so she just let out a huff of annoyance and went back to sleep.

As it turned out, though, I was right.

I was deep into the story of a serial killer when Mikaela and Jasmine burst into the room.

"Wait until you hear what we found out," Mikaela exclaimed. "I can't believe we didn't think to ask him sooner."

I didn't respond, too absorbed in the story I was reading.

"Kasi!"

I jolted and looked up at them. "What?"

"You have to listen to this," Jasmine said.

"But I was right in the middle of—"

"Seriously, you're going to want to know this!" Mikaela burst out.

"Okay, okay, tell me."

Jasmine settled on her bed and Mikaela began to pace.

"We were in Monsters Throughout History and I suddenly realized we had an expert on monsters right there in front of us and none of us had ever asked him. So I did. I went up to Professor Sommerland and I asked."

"Asked him what?"

"I asked who he thinks the Shadow Killer is."

I blanched. "In class?" I was horrified. What if the other students figured things out? What if it got back to Jahrdran that my roommates were asking about the shadow killer?

"Of course not! I waited until after class, then I asked him."

"Okay. And?"

"He doesn't know."

I rolled my eyes. "Of course, he doesn't." I went back to my book, determined to finish—

"But he doesn't think it was a shadow monster."

I froze and looked back up. "He doesn't?"

"Nope."

"Then who does he think it was?"

"He doesn't know, but he said it didn't make sense for it to be a shadow monster because they were known the world over for their heroic acts, using the shadows to leap into disaster areas to save lives."

"How did you explain even knowing about them?"

"I told him I'd run across a reference

to the killer while researching for his class, but I hadn't heard of the monster classification before and I was curious."

"Okay, well, while that's interesting, I don't see how it can help us."

"He also said the reason everyone believed the killer was a shadow monster was because only they can shadow-walk," Jasmine said.

"Yeah, except that wasn't entirely true," Mikaela's voice rose with her excitement. "According to Professor Sommerland, the mates of shadow monsters could also shadow-walk."

I nodded. "That's how I was able to pull Jahrdran into the shadows. Because he's my mate."

"Exactly and once a mate has access to the shadow realm, Mr. Sommerland said their access became permanent, and over time, they got better at shadow-walking."

"So he thinks maybe the killer was a shadow beast's mate?"

"It's the only other possibility, he said."

"Shit," I whispered.

"What?"

"Hold on, it's in here somewhere." I flipped back several pages, scanned, flipped a page again, then exclaimed, "Okay, listen to this."

"Wait!" Mikaela exclaimed. "Is that the history book? The one you've been trying to read forever?"

I nodded impatiently. "Something happened. I don't know how or why, but the copyright is now this year and there are hundreds of new pages at the end of the book."

"That must be the enchantment I could feel every time I touched it," Jasmine exclaimed. "We figured it was to keep non-shadow-monsters from reading it, but it must also have some sort of generation spell to it. I'm guessing when you touched it, Kasi, the spell was triggered to update the history within its pages."

"Which hopefully means it's an *objective* history that we can trust," I said.

"Right," Mikaela said. "It may also be why it's been so hard for you to read. Objectivity probably translates to a bunch of boring facts."

"Well, they're not so boring anymore,"

I said. "Listen to this. 'An execution order was handed down in 1810, condemning all shadow-beasts to death. The Varulvka were called in to carry out that order.

"'The prevailing theory among the shadow-beasts was that the extermination effort was either being led or manipulated by the rogue monsters themselves. At the time, the only viable threat to their reign of terror was the shadow-beasts, who now had to flee for their lives, leaving the hunt for the Shadow Killer unfinished. It was this development that had the shadow-beasts concerned the other supernaturals were being manipulated into acting against their own interests. Deaths reached an all-time high as the hunters became the hunted.

"'The shadow-beasts knew if the execution order was successfully carried out and they were eliminated, there would be no one left able to search the Shadows for the Killer."

I looked up. "First of all, I'd just like to point out the use of the term shadow-beast when every professor I've met has referred to me as a Monster. Maybe they're one and the same, but somehow Monster feels worse than Beast.

"Anyway, that's not the point. Imagine if Professor Sommerland is right and it *was* a mate. The shadow-beasts believed whoever the killer was, he or she had somehow influenced the decision to hunt them all."

"But it that were true, if the killer

was a mate, then he or she would be condemning their own mate to death," Mikaela protested.

"Where's the book about shadow-mates?"

Jasmine leaned over the foot of her bed and grabbed it off her bookshelf.

"Does it say anything about what happens when one of the mated pair dies?"

Jasmine flipped to a page she'd marked with a post-it and read out loud, "'Of all the mated bonds in the supernatural world, shadow-mates are the most likely to die within seconds of one another. Even shadow-mates who failed to complete their bond before their deaths have still passed together.'" She looked up. "I marked it because it's important for you to understand how tied you and Jahrdran are, even though he rejected you."

I wasn't ready to even think about that, so I ignored the comment and focused on finding the next passage I wanted to read them.

"'Okay, here it is. 'The shadow-beasts spent two years hunting the criminal known as the Shadow Killer. During those years, the number of deaths and disappearances grew by the millions.

"'While the shadow-beasts hunted, their chosen representative, Lydrel Zowen, the ambassador for the Council of Shadows, attempted to convince the other rulers that all shadow-beasts should not be condemned for the actions of one or even a few.'

"There's a footnote at the bottom of the page. It says, 'Lydrel Zowen was not a shadow-beast, but instead, was the dragon mate of Celia Warren, a shadow-beast who died of a rare, genetic disease. Zowen is the only known shadow-mate in history who did not succumb to death upon his mate's demise.

"Though watched carefully, there were no signs of mental deterioration or loss of control in Zowen following his mate's death, and in the years that followed, he focused his energy on his political career and climbed the ranks to become ambassador for the Council of Shadows.'"

I looked up. "What if they were wrong?"

"Wrong about what?" Mikaela asked.

"What if Zowen did go insane after his mate's death and *he's* the killer? Think about it. He would have had access to the shadow realm *and* he was in a position of power. He could have been the one behind the scenes, manipulating the supernatural community into issuing the Order of Execution in the first place."

Silence fell as the three of us contemplated that theory.

"Okay, it's a solid theory," Mikaela said, "but how do we go about proving something that happened hundreds of years ago?"

"It's like trying to solve the coldest cold case in supernatural history," Jasmine said.

"Especially if our only suspect is

dead," Mikaela said.

"Of course, he's dead," I said. "It's been hundreds of years!"

"Eh, well, you know," Jasmine said. "Some supernaturals are really long-lived."

"But surely not for *hundreds of years*?" I glanced from Jasmine to Mikaela, who simply shrugged and nodded. "So, how long do you guys live?" Before they could answer, I shook my head and waved a hand in the air. "Never mind. Don't answer that. I don't want to know. As far as I'm concerned, we're all going to live forever."

They both laughed.

"That works for me," Mikaela said.

"Yeah, me too." Jasmine grinned.

"Anyway," I said. "I'm going to try to

finish reading this chapter. Maybe you guys can go to the library and see if you can find out anything more about this guy." I leaned over and grabbed a notepad and pen from my nightstand. I scrawled a couple lines, tore off the top paper and handed it to Mikaela.

"Lydrel Zowen, dragon," she read out loud. "Celia Warren, shadow-beast."

"I doubt there's anything about her that will help us, since she died long before the Shadow Killer showed up, but just in case."

"We'll see what we can find out."

CHAPTER NINE

THE FOLLOWING WEEK was crazy. With end-of-semester exams approaching, we didn't have as much time for research as we wanted, and even when we did manage a few hours, we found nothing to help us in our quest for proof.

Meanwhile, every time I saw Jahrdran in the hallways, my heart would drop and pain would saturate my being.

MONSTER'S REWARD

Just like old times, I'd slide back into the shadows and he'd beast-out and go into hunting mode.

This time, though, he'd simply glare at whatever shadow I was sheltering in, as if he knew exactly where I was, before loping away, clearly furious his beast still wanted me.

I was too.

Furious that he'd rejected me.

By now, I was no longer crying myself to sleep at night, and was no longer going out of my way to avoid places I knew he'd be.

Why should I walk ten minutes in the opposite direction, taking the long way around the school, just to avoid that one hallway where I knew his class let out?

So what if he didn't like having to

scent me nearby?

This was on him and if I was going to be heartbroken, he could deal with the discomfort of knowing his rejected fated mate was nearby.

I still vacillated between anger and sorrow, but the anger was more prevalent now.

Exams came and went and I did a fairly decent showing, then the majority of the student body left the school to journey home for the holidays.

I, of course, with no family to visit, stayed behind.

Both Mikaela and Jasmine invited me to go home with them, but I turned them down.

It was nice to have been invited, but I was looking forward to continuing my research in the shadow-room.

I was dismayed to discover the day after the students left, that Jahrdran had stayed behind as well.

It was harder to avoid him when the halls were mostly empty and meals were still served on a schedule.

Every time I saw him, the rage inside me just grew.

Literally, everything about him reminded me of all that I'd lost.

Not just the loss of *him*, my fated mate, but also the loss of any knowledge of my family, my history, my culture, my own beast.

What other supernatural lived in complete and utter darkness about who they were and what they were capable of?

PEPPER MCGRAW

What other supernatural at this Academy had the professors literally working against them, actively attempting to prevent them from discovering their own history?

Everything came to a head mid-way through our semester break.

I'd just finished making myself a sandwich in the mess hall, when I turned and saw Jahrdran across the way, standing at the beverage station, serving himself one of his *special* energy drinks, made specifically to sharpen the senses and hunting instincts of the Varulvka.

Every single supernatural in the Academy had a special beverage created just for their kind. Everyone but me, that is.

No one could serve me the Drink of Shades, for it required access to ingredients only found in the shadow realm.

I knew this because I'd found a cookbook in the shadow-room titled *Recipes from the Shadows.* In it, I had found several *special* drinks, intended only for shadow-beasts. Unfortunately, they weren't on offer at the Academy for obvious reasons.

Regardless, it made me furious to see Jahrdran standing alone by the beverage station, serving himself in a way that I never could.

Setting down my tray on a table nearby, I stalked over to stand at his side. "Must be nice to come from a long line of sanctioned killers."

PEPPER MCGRAW

His knuckles went white where they were holding the glass and fur rippled along his arm.

He carefully set his glass down, then turned to face me. "What the fuck do you want?"

I drew in a deep breath, making a concerted effort to calm my racing heart. "I just think it's interesting, don't you? A shadow killer stalked the realms and killed millions. For that, an entire species of shadow-beasts were sentenced to death. Your people, the Varulvka, hunted them down, presumably killing millions in the process. Yet *those* kills were sanctioned, and therefore, your people were heroes. And all for committing genocide against a species that may not have been guilty of the crimes they were accused of."

"What the fuck are you talking about?" he growled. "Of course, they were guilty."

"Were they? Was there any evidence? Did they ever figure out which shadow-beast committed the crimes?"

"It didn't matter which one, the fact that they could access the shadow realm at all meant they were guilty."

"*One* was guilty. *One* individual who could access the shadow realm. That doesn't necessarily say shadow-beast to me."

"Shadow-*Monster*," he corrected me.

"So says the victor. It's another way to wash away the truth, to obscure the facts. Paint an entire species as monsters, then execute them for crimes they never committed."

"You don't know that."

"I know the majority—we'll call them *millions*—of those executed were innocent. I know that the *one* they were hunting may not have been a shadow-beast at all and even if he was, it didn't justify the genocide that followed. The victims literally became as bad as the killer they were hunting."

He sighed. "Why are we even having this conversation, Kasi?"

"Because I know you're wrong. I know *they* were wrong. And I know the real killer has gotten away with murder ever since." I turned and walked away.

That last sentence wasn't really true. I didn't *know* that, but after all my research and everything that I'd read, I wasn't convinced the killer was dead.

I'd learned a lot about the shadows since finding the shadow-room and the most important thing I'd learned was how much of a dichotomy they were.

For those not born of the shadows, death was all that waited for them there. When thrown into them, they had a tiny window of time, no more than thirty minutes in length, during which they might escape with some of their inner light intact.

Depending on the strength of the person, their light might only survive a moment or the full thirty, but after they passed that time threshold, whatever it might be, there would be no light left to guide them through the endless dark, and they would be lost forever, their souls now twisted and dark.

For the shadow-born, however, the shadows represented both life *and* death. The shadow realm could heal the physical form, but that required re-entry into the physical world.

If re-entry did not happen, if a shadow-beast lingered too long in the shadows, they could lose their physical form entirely, doomed to roam the realms as nothing more than shadow and mist.

I couldn't help but wonder if this had become the fate of the many hunted who had fled into the shadows to avoid persecution.

And if that were the case, it was only reasonable to also wonder if somewhere hiding within the shadow realm lay the remnants of a killer, waiting for his chance to kill again.

A clatter broke into my thoughts and Jahrdran dropped into the seat across from me, his tray of food in front of him.

I raised an eyebrow, trying not to show my joy at having my mate join me for lunch.

"Why do you think the killer is still out there?"

I shrugged. "Why do you think he's not?"

"For the love of—Kasi, if you're wasting my time—" he glared at me, his voice a guttural growl, sending both dread and heat washing over me in equal measure.

"If it's the last thing I do, I'm going to solve this case," I said to him. "If it was a shadow-beast, I'll prove it. If it was some other monster—a Varulvka, perhaps—"

He let out a low, rumbling growl that echoed through the empty cafeteria.

"I'll prove that as well."

"A Varulvka would never—"

"Really? Because your kind are hunters. They're natural-born killers. Shadow-beasts on the other hand—do you even know what their calling was before they were condemned?"

Jahrdran looked confused. "Why would I care?"

"Because they were firefighters, paramedics, hospital workers. They used the shadows to leap into disaster areas to stage rescue attempts. Do you know how dangerous it is to leap from one shadow to another that you cannot see?

MONSTER'S REWARD

Do you know how dangerous it is to take a leap into the unknown and pray that where you land, there will be enough shadow to hold your form together, especially if you're in an entirely different time zone and can't be certain if there will be enough light to cast a shadow at all?

"The shadow-beasts trained their entire lives to *risk* those lives shadow-walking to save others. They were *not* monsters and they were *not* killers."

"How the hell do you know this?"

I smiled at him. "Because I'm a phenomenal researcher."

"Don't be ridiculous. There's absolutely no mention of Shadow-Monsters anywhere in our Academy library. I know because I've searched."

"If that's true, how would you know about what your people did to mine? You yourself said it happened hundreds of years before you were born."

"Because what happened to the shadow monsters is part of the historical records of the Varulvka. The oath our leaders took on behalf of the Varulvka—" He hesitated.

"What oath?" I asked.

He sighed. "The oath to hunt down every shadow monster in existence. That oath destroyed an entire generation of elite hunters. They did their duty and when they were done, they self-destructed. *All* of them. Most self-terminated, others simply curled up and died, still others drank themselves to death. Do you know how hard it is for a supernatural to drink themselves to death?"

I shook my head.

"It takes true dedication. I suppose it's just a longer way to self-terminate."

"So what you're saying is that even then, the Varulvka knew it was wrong to carry out their oath, but they did it anyway."

"Do you understand how a supernatural oath works? It has no end date, which means it works on *every* Varulvka hunter in every timeline. So long as we believed the shadow monsters were all gone from the realm, the oath was quiet. But now that I know there's a shadow monster alive, the oath is working on me right now, raking against my skin, boiling in my organs, an absolute *compulsion* to snuff you out of existence. The only thing saving you is our fated mate bond. Its need to protect you is stronger than the compulsion to kill you." He glared at me. "For now anyway."

"So it's uncomfortable to resist the oath. Who the fuck cares?" I hissed. "I'm sure it was a hell of a lot *more* uncomfortable for the ones who died. Your people should have resisted, *especially* since the Killer himself is probably the one who recommended the Order of Execution in the first place."

Jahrdran looked horrified. "There's no way. There were no shadow monsters advising any of the paranormals who made that decision."

"No. But there was the mate of one,

the mate of a shadow-beast who had died four years before."

"How the hell do you know that?"

"What makes you think the Varulvka were the only ones who kept their records intact? There was at least one other species who had as much to lose as the Varulvka."

"Are you seriously trying to imply you've gained access to shadow-monster records?"

"Shadow-*beast*, if you don't mind. And this *is* the Academy of Secrets, full of hidden rooms and passages, is it not?

"That's just a rumor."

"So you *haven't* discovered any secret areas in the three years you've been a student here?"

He hesitated.

"Exactly."

"Yes, but it doesn't make any sense that you would find *shadow* information in any of those places."

"It does if you assume once upon a time, Blackthorn Academy had shadow-beast professors *and* students. After all, the school's been enrolling students since the late 1600s."

"Show me these secret rooms and passages."

"Not a chance."

He let out a low growl of annoyance.

"But I'll show you a couple of my books."

CHAPTER TEN

IT WAS A terrible idea to bring Jahrdran to my room. I knew it, even as he followed me up the five flights of stairs.

Sure, I could have shadow-walked my way up them, but walking the old-fashioned way gave me a chance to think.

I reviewed the books currently in my room, debating which ones I wanted to show him—and the ones I didn't—and worrying about which ones might be lying in plain sight.

When I'd first started bringing books up to our room, we'd kept them hidden from prying eyes, just in case. However, as the weeks had passed and no one seemed to notice that I was constantly carting books back and forth from the basement, we'd gotten a little lazy.

Now, I was pretty sure I'd left at least one of the books open on my bed. I just couldn't remember which one.

I then tried to picture the book and was pretty sure it was lying face-up, pages exposed, which made me wonder whether it was *A History of Shadows* and if so, whether the pages would be blank. After all, Jahrdran wasn't a shadow-beast, so theoretically, he shouldn't be able to read the book, just like Jasmine and Mikaela couldn't.

Except, he was also my mate, which could mean he'd have access to shadow secrets the way he had access to the shadow realm.

As we climbed, I became increasingly aware of the beast stalking at my back.

Shadow raced ahead of us, happily jumping up several steps, then swiveling to make sure we were following her.

She was absolutely thrilled that Jahrdran was speaking to us again, even though I wasn't sure he really was.

There was a lot left unsaid and he was a seething mass of emotions at my back.

For all I knew, he was following me upstairs to kill me.

MONSTER'S REWARD

My step faltered at that thought, but I powered through, refusing to believe things were that dire.

We finally reached my room and I led the way inside.

I crossed the room and climbed onto my bed, propping my back against the wall, then waited to see whether he would choose a desk chair, Jasmine's bed or to sit next to me on mine.

He chose a desk chair.

We stared at each other in silence for a few moments, then he said, "Books."

Right. I debated a long moment, then finally said, "Behind you."

He swiveled in the chair and saw the stack of books on the desk behind him. He looked through them silently, then glanced at me. "Where'd you get all these?"

"I told you. There are secrets at Blackthorn and I've discovered a few."

"How do you even know these are authentic?"

I rolled my eyes. "Trust me. I found them in a place only another shadow-beast could access."

"Have you read them all?"

"Not all of them."

He opened one of the books, then scowled. "The pages are blank."

I winced. "Some of the books only work for shadow-beasts." I leaned forward to see the title and tried not to show my relief that the book had wisely hidden its wisdom from him.

I would hate to be the shadow-beast who gave away all our secrets to the enemy and I had no doubt *A Shadow-Beast's Guide to the Shadow Realm* held many of our secrets. And no matter his status as my mate, the reality was Jahrdran was a Varulvka, and the Varulvka, as our executioners, would always be the enemies of the shadow-beasts.

"Try a different one," I urged him.

He reached for the next book in the stack, which happened to be *The Dangers of the Shadow Realm.* That book wasn't cooperative either.

It took three more attempts before the books finally showed him some text, and it was *Shadow-Mates.*

He glared at me in disgust.

I shrugged. "Look, I can't help it. The books have minds of their own. They probably thought you could use some tips on being a better mate."

He growled low in his throat, tossed the book back on the desk and lunged across the room at me. "I'll show you a better mate."

He had me flat on my back on the bed in an instant, came down over me and claimed my mouth with his.

Heat instantly barreled through me.

He settled his weight over me, pressing me deeper into the mattress.

I wrapped my legs around his waist and my arms around his neck and tried to get closer, all the while kissing him frantically.

He leaned back, just enough to give him room to rake his claws through the seam of my shirt and rip it from my torso.

As he was ripping my shirt to shreds, I was struggling to rid him of his.

As my shirt fell away, he surged upward and finished the job of yanking his own shirt over his head. He then set one claw against my belly button and slowly dragged it upward.

It caught on my bra and with one quick yank, he tore the bra into two sections that fell to either side.

My girls fell free and he settled both hands over them, squeezing gently.

I arched my back and gasped.

He leaned back and with a couple more slashes of his claws, had us both naked.

He slowly settled back over me and the feel of my mate, lying on top of me, skin-to-skin, had tears burning in my eyes.

I lunged upward, wrapping my arms around his shoulders and burying my face in his neck. "Jahrdran." I set my teeth against his pulse, a beat I felt in every pore of my body, and scraped gently.

He let out a muted roar, notched his cock at my entrance and pressed forward.

I let out a low hiss at the burn and stretch and glorious ache as he slowly inched his way inside.

"Jahrdran," I whimpered, everything in me lighting up at the feel of my mate pressing deep.

"Kasi," he growled, pulling back, then surging forward again, lighting fires in his wake.

He began to power inside me, over and over again, and I met him thrust for thrust, desperate to get closer, to make this moment last an eternity or longer.

As I dragged him down for a ravenous kiss, a quiver began deep inside, then grew to a massive quake, one that shook me from the inside out, that swelled until it seemed it might shatter the world, then hung there, for endless, breathless moments.

The world disappeared in an explosion of light and in that moment, nothing existed but the two of us and the desperate, shattering quake that rolled us beneath its powerful, endless waves.

Long moments passed as I lay there,

pulse throbbing in tune to the tiny aftershocks that constantly rippled through me, causing my core to flutter around him.

Jahrdran's weight settled more fully over me, his fangs buried in my neck, his heart pounding in sync with my own. His cock stretched me to overflowing still, its knot swollen to almost unbearable proportions.

I sifted the fingers of one hand through his hair, scratching his scalp with my nails, while stroking my other hand up and down his back in a slow caress, reveling in the feel of my mate.

Slowly our heartbeats settled to a more normal rhythm and our breathing evened out.

Still, the knot remained, locking him

inside me.

"Jahrdran," I murmured his name, so thankful he'd come back to me.

As if the sound of my voice broke some sort of spell, he stiffened in my arms, then unclamped his jaws from my neck, his fangs retracting slowly.

He sucked on the wound there for a moment, sealing it closed with his saliva, then pushed himself up.

We were still locked together, so he didn't try to extract himself, but he definitely seemed to want some distance.

"Jahrdran?"

A muscle twitched along his jawline, then he slowly lowered his head so our eyes met.

"What is it?" I reached up to brush his hair out of his eyes, but he jerked his head to the side at the last minute and I allowed my hand to fall at my side, a strange clenching around my heart catching my breath and holding it hostage.

"This was a mistake." His voice was rough and gravely and pain-filled.

His unhappiness at what he was saying was as clear as mine, so why was he insisting on saying it?

"It wasn't," I said emphatically. "We're fated mates. We're *supposed* to be together."

He shook his head. "My oath is telling me to kill you right now. That you're vulnerable and this is the moment to strike. It *hurts* to resist." He glared down at me, as if I was somehow responsible for his suffering.

I suppose, in a way, I was.

"I'm sorry, but we'll figure it out."

He shook his head. "No, Kasi, we won't." He slowly pulled out, his knot having finally subsided, perhaps in response to the oath's resurgence, and climbed off me.

He stalked toward the door.

"Wait. Aren't we going to talk? Make a plan?"

"The only plan I have is to avoid you," he snarled, reaching for the door.

"Don't you think you should get dressed first?"

He yanked open the door and stormed through it, shifting into his beast as he went.

I jumped from the bed, yanked the sheet around me and hurried to the door. By the time I got there, he was nowhere to be seen.

CHAPTER ELEVEN

TWO DAYS LATER, Jahrdran plopped down next to me in the cafeteria. He straddled the bench so he was facing me.

Shadow, who was stretched out in the shadows beneath the lunch table, immediately perked up and inched closer to him.

Traitor.

She turned and rubbed up against

my legs, winding around them before heading back to him.

Still a traitor.

Miss him. She set her head on his lap and he scratched between her ears.

I know, baby. Me too, but he's a jerk and doesn't deserve to know we miss him.

Yes. She tipped back her head and nipped his fingers.

He hissed and pulled them back, giving her a wide-eyed look.

She responded with a purr and rubbed her head against his thighs again.

I snickered.

He glared at me. "You turned your cat against me."

"Please, you did that yourself by

rejecting your mate. *Twice.*"

He let out a soft growl of frustration.

I clenched my jaw against the urge to grin and side-eyed him. "So why are you here?"

"I've spent the past two days researching online and it's a bigger cluster than I thought."

I rolled my eyes. "Of course, it is. That's what happens when people are sheep."

This time his growl was neither low nor soft.

"I found out something too," I announced. It was true. I did.

Having Jahrdran walk out a second time had been a blow I wasn't prepared for, so I'd taken a break from the huge tomes of history and philosophy and culture and had turned to the shadow-kitten care book.

I learned so much, I wished I'd started with that book.

"Did you know that a shadow-kitten is born when a shadow-beast is?"

"Makes sense, seeing as the history books only mention one shadow-kitten per monster."

"So what happens is a shadow-beast is born and within hours of his or her birth, the parents take the infant into the shadow realm to find their shadow-kitten. The two are inseparable from that moment on.

"Except my parents didn't exactly stick around after my birth. Within a few hours, I was abandoned at a human hospital and thus began my life as a human.

"Fast-forward twenty-plus years and I discover I'm a supernatural with the ability to shadow-walk and what do you know? I also have a shadow-kitten who's been waiting in the shadow realm her entire life for me to show up and set her free.

"Only I didn't know to do that, now did I? Because when I arrived here, none of the professors were willing to tell me much of anything at all and so I continued blindly in the dark, trying to figure things out, and by a sheer stroke of luck, managed to slip into the shadow realm and leave a trail for Shadow to follow.

"That's what my life's been like, Jahrdran. A series of events that have kept me in the dark or by sheer luck, revealed a truth.

"Now I'm deliberately searching for that truth and no one's going to stand in my way, not even my fated mate. So don't go burying your head in the sand about your people and their role in the fiasco that is my life."

I turned in my seat and glared at him.

We were so close, I could lean forward and kiss him so easily. Tempting, but not the task at hand. "So, let's hear it. What truths have you uncovered?"

"Once the shadow-beasts were all gone from the world, things got dark for the Varulvka."

"Oh, they got dark for the victors in that battle? How sad for *your* people."

Yes, I sounded bitter, but so what? I *deserved* to be bitter. What was wrong with the world back then that genocide seemed the answer?

Jahrdran sighed. "Look, I'm just telling you what was recorded in our historical records. Don't blame the messenger."

"Fine. Go on."

"The elite hunters who had carried out the Execution Order started dying, either by their own hand or by sheer reckless folly or by misadventure of some sort. There were so many deaths, the Council instigated a wave of investigations to make sure there was no foul play involved.

"What they found was an entire generation of elite hunters in a crisis of conscience for being forced to do something they were opposed to in every way. There were records, journal entries, meetings with therapists, letters written to loved ones and the theme that emerged over and over again was their devastation and guilt over their participation in the persecution of millions."

"So they developed a conscience," I said bitterly, "but entirely too late for the ones they killed."

"There's nothing in the records to make me believe this, but they're so carefully worded that I came to the conclusion that many of the Varulvka fought the oath long enough to help groups of Shadow-Monsters flee. I'm not positive, but I believe it's possible that some, if not all of the self-terminations, were because there were *still* monsters to be hunted, but as long as no one knew about them, the oath would die with the Varulvka."

"So where are they? If there are some Shadow-Monsters still alive, if the Varulvka truly helped some escape, where are they?"

"I don't know, but it gives me hope."

"Why?"

"Because if those long-ago Varulvka could ignore their oaths in order to help strangers they didn't even know, surely I can do the same to avoid killing my mate."

"They did it by killing *themselves*, Jahrdran!"

"Yes, well, obviously, I'd like to avoid

that result."

I stared at him.

This was the first time in the past two months that he'd given any indication that he might be willing to try.

I wasn't going to lose that chance.

"So, what's the plan?" I asked him.

"Well, first of all, I think we need to conduct a thorough investigation of the list of suspects I found."

"You found a list of suspects?"

"I did. The Council kept careful records of every step involved, from the moment they first realized there was a killer hunting from the shadows, to the very end, when shadow monsters and their hunters were all gone.

"There was chaos for quite some time in the aftermath, at least until the next generation of Varulvka managed to grow into their powers. Unfortunately—" He hesitated.

"There was no next generation of shadow monsters to act as public servants and heroes, so the world had to go on without them."

"Exactly. The Varulvka Council looked around and realized what exactly had been wrought by their decision to accept the Hunter's Oath for an entire species. This is a story every young Varulvka studies, so that they understand both the potential power and the potential horror in taking an oath. We learn that even now, generations later, we are still bound by that oath.

"The Council spent a lot of time investigating every supernatural who signed the Execution Order naming the Varulvka as the Hunters of Record. They also investigated anyone close to those who signed it. They eventually narrowed that list to three suspects.

"Don't tell me. One of those is a shadow-beast's dragon mate."

"Yep. The other two were an unmated witch and an unmated necromancer."

I nodded. "Because maybe they had an incomplete mate bond with a Shadow-Beast who died."

"Exactly." He hesitated, then, "Look, Kasi, I know it's tempting to hang your hopes on one of these three suspects, but there's no guarantee. It could as easily have been a shadow–" He caught himself, then finished, "–*beast.*"

"I know, but I'm going to do

everything I can to prove otherwise."

"Then I guess I'm in as well."

The rush of hope that swept through me left me dizzy. "Really?"

He nodded. "Let's go look at some more books." He stood and held out his hand.

I stared at it a moment, then slowly set my hand in his, and allowed him to pull me to my feet.

We dumped our trays as we exited the cafeteria, and on our way out, I caught a glimpse of the head table.

Most of the professors had gone home for the holidays, but a few had stayed behind and they were staring at the two of us, concern written all over their faces.

"Did you see Professors Dewar and

Sommerland staring at us?"

"Eh, that's not quite so concerning as the look on the Headmistress' face when she saw us sitting together. She turned right around and left again."

"I didn't see that. They're going to forbid me from talking with you, I just know it."

"Give me a break. They can't keep us apart. We're fated mates."

My heart skipped a beat at hearing him acknowledge that, but I didn't comment. Instead, I just said, "That's not going to make a bit of difference considering they know what we are."

"I've been thinking about that. You're sure they know?"

"Of course, I am. They've been teaching me to control my shadow skills in private." Not that I'd learned that much about the shadows from them. It had taken breaking into the archive room and finding my people's secret library to do that.

"Let's go to the basement," I said, abruptly switching directions, leading him down the stairs. "I've already looked through every book I have upstairs. I need to search again."

"You're finally going to show me your secret room?"

"No. We're going to the library to see what we can find out there."

He rolled his eyes. "There's nothing in the library, Kasi. There's not a single reference to Shadow Monsters."

"No, but now that we have an actual list of suspects, I'm thinking some normal research in the library, trying to get more information on them, is in order." Depending on what we found there, I might just show him my shadow-room after, but I wasn't ready to commit to that yet.

"Makes sense, I guess, but I have to say, it's rather suspicious, don't you think, that there's literally *nothing* about shadow monsters in the entire library? I mean, this *is* an academic institution. They shouldn't be censoring anything, no matter what their orders are. I'm also wondering why they didn't just turn you in to the Varulvka Council from the very beginning."

I whirled on him, glaring.

He raised his hands. "I'm not saying they *should* have. I'm just saying if they didn't, they must know more than they're saying."

"Of course, they do! In fact, I'm quite sure they know a lot, but they've refused to share. Every time I've asked why my people were killed, they've told me the past is past and I should worry about the future. If you think I haven't asked, about a million times, you're crazy." I started to push the library door open, then froze as Headmistress Blackthorn's voice reached us.

"Are you absolutely positive there's not a single reference to the shadow monsters anywhere in this library?"

"Headmistress, we've run countless spells, hunting down every tiny instance when they were mentioned." That was Mr. Brecken's voice. "There's nothing left."

"Then why did I just see Kasi Smith having lunch with Jahrdran Vilnik?"

"Did you? Interesting. Perhaps they have an assignment together."

"They're in completely different years and don't have a single class together."

"Well, the castle is fairly empty at this point. Perhaps it's simply coincidence."

"As if I believe in coincidences. No. This is something more. Their body language was disturbingly intimate. We cannot risk them becoming friends. It's the fastest way for Kasi to discover the truth."

"My dear, Ophelia."

I startled because *that* wasn't Mr. Brecken's voice. It was Professor Dunlop's.

Jahrdran turned toward me and mouthed, "The dean of students?"

I nodded.

"It's been over two hundred years," Professor Dunlop continued. "Even though most supernaturals think the shadow monsters are a myth, I'd be surprised if one of the Varulvka believed it and Kasi already knows the truth. So, what exactly are you afraid of her discovering?"

After a long silence, during which I tried desperately to hear anything they might be saying, Mr. Brecken said, "Ah. You do not want her to know that her people were slaughtered in vain."

I staggered, my knees buckling from hearing it stated so plainly, and Jahrdran set a stabilizing hand on my hip, drawing me into his side, a move that was as surprising as it was comforting.

"Oh, don't be ridiculous, Mr. Brecken," Professor Dunlop exclaimed. "Just because the council no longer believes the shadow-beast was the killer doesn't mean they're right."

"It doesn't matter whether they're right or not," the Headmistress said. "The point is it would be devastating for Kasi to know it's even a possibility. Worse, though, would be if the boy Jahrdran found out. The Varulvka are fierce hunters, but they are also profoundly tied to the concepts of honor and justice. To discover how far from those ideals they fell would be devastating. We *must* protect our students, even when it means keeping the truth of their pasts from them."

"What if they're fated mates?" Mr. Brecken asked. "You did say they appeared intimate."

"I sincerely hope that isn't the case," Headmistress Blackthorn said.

"Yes," Professor Dunlop agreed. "That would be a true tragedy seeing as he is bound by the oath of his people to hunt all known shadow-beasts to extinction."

"As long as he's unaware of her true nature, she should be safe enough," Mr. Brecken said.

"Is there no way to break the oath?" Professor Dunlop asked.

"There's only one way that I know of," the Headmistress said, "and that's to prove a shadow-beast wasn't the Shadow

Killer, after all."

I was shaking and couldn't stop.

I wanted to storm inside the library and rage at the Headmistress and the Dean and even the librarian, but I knew it wasn't their fault.

They weren't the ones who had signed the execution order, nor had they hunted my kind into extinction for a crime everyone now seemed to agree they hadn't committed in the first place.

The only thing the professors were guilty of was trying to protect me and my mate.

I turned and caught sight of the look on Jahrdran's face.

If I was furious and sick, it was nothing compared to what was happening with him.

PEPPER MCGRAW

His face was ashen and his brilliant, blue eyes were glistening with tears.

His wolf ears were laying flat on his head, fur was sprouting everywhere and his fists were clenched, claws out, blood pooling where they pierced his skin.

It wasn't as if we'd heard anything different from what we'd just been discussing. The problem for Jahrdran, though, was that even though he'd agreed to help, he hadn't really believed my theory until now.

That much was obvious from the look on his face.

Unfortunately, hearing our professors stating out loud that even the council no longer believed the shadow-beasts were guilty, Jahrdran could no longer deny the truth of our history and the reality of that was finally slamming home.

Worse yet was hearing that his oath would remain in place until we solved this mystery for his people and for mine.

Now more concerned about my mate and his state of mind than continuing our research, I stepped into his space, slid an arm around his waist and led him away from the library.

We walked up six flights of stairs silently, both lost in our own thoughts.

I took him to my room, where we curled up on my bed and simply held each other as day fell to night.

We didn't talk about it the next day.

Jahrdran murmured that he had some more research to do and left me.

Again.

For the third time.

This time, I forgave him, though.

His entire world view had just been altered and he now had to come to terms with the fact that everything his people *and* mine had suffered had been in vain.

As for me, it was hard to feel empathy for the people who had slaughtered mine, but having witnessed Jahrdran's ashen response, I could only imagine how much harder it had to have been for the original hunters when they realized they were hunting innocents, but were bound by an oath to execute them anyway.

I spent the rest of our break continuing to read the *History of Shadows* and perusing the shelves of the shadow-room for more books.

Unfortunately, the readings did

nothing to dispel the theory that the Shadow Killer could still be out there. In fact, I ended the book convinced the killer was still wreaking havoc across the known universes.

It was that last weekend, when students were starting to arrive back at the castle, that I found *The Book of Shadows*.

It was on the bottom shelf in the shadow-room, hidden at the very back, as if it had fallen from a higher shelf, sliding down a wall made of shadows.

I opened it and immediately knew the explanation for my existence was probably somewhere inside that weighty tome, for it appeared to be a complete record of shadow-beast lineages for the past five hundred years.

PEPPER MCGRAW

When I arrived back in our room, Mikaela and Jasmine had arrived and were waiting for an update on anything I'd discovered while they were gone.

We spent hours talking, both of them shocked but excited to hear that Jahrdran was starting to come around.

Eventually, Jasmine went off in search of snacks and caffeine while Mikaela and I got back into the research.

Mikaela was stretched out on Jasmine's bed, reading about shadow-mates, and I was flipping through *The Book of Shadows*, examining family trees and shadow-beast lineages, when it happened.

In our earlier research, we had discovered that the shadow realm could heal shadow-beasts to the extent that they could potentially live forever, but that if they stayed too long in the shadow realm without visiting the physical world, they risked dissolving into nothing but shadows themselves.

In the lineages, there were shadow-beasts who had lived for hundreds of years and others who had no dates of death recorded. I was wondering whether those without a death date had fled into the shadows to avoid persecution, and if so, whether they had dissolved to mist by now, when Jasmine's side of the room erupted in shadows.

Shadow let out a snarl and lunged across the room, tackling one of the long, smoky-gray tentacles that had surrounded Mikaela.

PEPPER MCGRAW

The tentacles tightened around her, then bucked as if in an attempt to dislodge Shadow, before vanishing in an instant, taking Mikaela and Shadow with them.

I lunged across the room, my shadow-beast exploding from me, but there were no shadows to enter.

They had all disappeared.

I whirled and dove under my bed, sliding into the shadows waiting there.

CHAPTER TWELVE

THE SPACE UNDER my bed had always seemed larger than it looked, and now that I understood the magic of the shadows and how they all led to the shadow realm for those able to enter it, I no longer considered the underside of my bed to be fully of this world anymore.

Instead, it was a gateway to the shadow realm.

Even so, whenever I went beneath my

bed, I pretty much stayed within that small, though larger than it appeared, pocket of space.

Until now, I had never attempted to explore beyond it and I had no real idea of what to expect.

The real world, like always, seemed so close, the bed still above me and our dorm room behind me.

If I retreated, I knew I'd crawl right out from under the bed back into my room.

So I crawled forward, toward the wall that stretched alongside my bed, then past where it should be into a vast open space of shadows.

Shadow? I reached for the path that connected Shadow and me and hoped she would hear my call.

No answer.

I climbed to my feet and started walking.

Shadow! I tried to increase the volume of my telepathic call, but it's hard to shout in your mind when there's no real sound to your voice.

Kasi. The voice was faint, but I heard it.

Shadow, I'm here. Where are you?

Kasi.

Keep talking. I'll find you.

Kasi, hurry. He's hurting Mikaela. Her voice was getting louder, so I told myself I must be going in the right direction, even though as far as I could tell, I wasn't getting anywhere fast.

The shadows around me didn't waver and everything looked the same.

MONSTER'S REWARD

Even though I was used to going in and out of the shadow realm regularly, and in fact, had spent a huge amount of time in the shadow-room over the past couple months, this shadow-pocket of the shadow realm did not feel welcoming like all those other spaces did.

Instead, it felt menacing and dark, and the further into the realm I traveled, the darker and more foreboding it seemed.

Kasi, hurry!

At that moment, the silence was broken by a shrill scream.

Chills ran down my back as I recognized that voice. Mikaela!

I raced toward the screams that seemed to echo around me as the shadows got darker and darker.

PEPPER MCGRAW

I burst through a particularly dense shadow and there they were.

Mikaela was being held in place by dark shadows that were seething all around her, seeping into her skin and slithering from her pores.

She screamed again and writhed in place, pinned in mid-air by nothing but those damn shadow-tentacles.

Her skin rippled and a leopard came snarling free, then disappeared, sinking back into her skin.

"Mikaela!" I ran forward, but fire erupted all around her, then the leopard appeared again.

Some of the shadows wrapped around her struggled with others and it took a moment for me to realize it was Shadow.

MONSTER'S REWARD

She was clawing and raking at the shadow-tentacles, dragging them away from Mikaela, but every time she got one away, another attacked.

Mikaela's skin rippled again and her leopard let out a pained roar that shook the shadow realm with its power.

The shadows covering her, all but Shadow herself, withdrew for a split second.

Seeing my chance, I leapt forward, exploding into my shadow-beast form.

I wrapped my shadows, those tentacles I'd used to kill three men a lifetime ago, around Mikaela and Shadow, pictured the shadows of our closet back in our dorm room and *flung* us there from the shadow realm.

One moment, everything was gray,

the next we were staggering out of the closet.

My knees buckled and the three of us landed in a heap on our dorm room floor.

I heard Jahrdran and Jasmine's voices exclaiming our names, but my eyes felt weighted shut and my entire system was shutting down.

I wanted to warn them that we'd just been attacked by the shadows, to check on Shadow and Mikaela to see if they were all right, but I couldn't even twitch a finger, let alone open my eyes.

The world faded away.

***

I woke to the weight of Shadow on my chest and the feel of her claws batting at my hair.

Once again, I marveled at being able to feel her physical form when she was made entirely of shadows. However it happened, though, I loved waking each morning to her antics.

A moment later, memory exploded in my brain and my eyes flew open.

We were lying on a medical bed in the infirmary.

"Kasima," Jahrdran leaned over me and I realized he'd been sitting in a chair next to the bed, holding my hand. "Sweetness." He slid a hand behind my neck and kissed me.

A wave of heat rolled through me and I kissed him back.

I was only vaguely aware of Shadow grumbling in annoyance as she jumped down from the bed.

Jahrdran took immediate advantage and pressed closer, filling up the space where Shadow had been.

I lost all sense of place and time as his kiss consumed and set me ablaze.

Long moments passed before the sound of a throat clearing had us pulling apart.

Jasmine stood on the other side of my bed, looking worried.

The minute Jahrdran straightened, she flung herself at me and hugged me tight. "I was so worried you weren't going to wake up."

I hugged her back, terrified to ask, but needing to know. "Mikaela?"

Jasmine stepped back and glanced to the side.

Mikaela was lying on a medical bed a couple feet away and she was not awake.

"She's in really bad shape," Jasmine said. "They're not sure she's going to make it and they're afraid to move her because she's been so unstable. She keeps flashing to her leopard form, then setting the bed on fire, but it doesn't really burn. It's like her powers are both stronger and weaker all at the same time."

Shit.

I sat up and went to climb out of the bed, but Jahrdran grabbed me by the shoulders. "Where are you going? You shouldn't be up yet, at least not until the nurse says you're okay."

"I'm fine, Jahrdran." I took a moment to really check in with my body and realized I wasn't lying. I actually felt incredible, full of energy and ready to take on the world. "Really. Let me up."

He stepped back, but hovered as I climbed from the bed, as if he was worried I would collapse.

I gave him a grin, dragged on my jeans, whipped the stupid hospital gown off me and pulled on my t-shirt. "Feeling great!" I gave a couple quick jumping jacks to prove it. "So, how long was I out?"

"You collapsed yesterday," Jasmine said.

"It's been almost twenty-four hours." Jahrdran's voice was rough and seeing the look on his face, I realized he was grappling with some pretty powerful emotions.

I stepped close and wrapped my arms around his waist, leaning into his chest.

His arms immediately closed around me in a tight hug. He dropped his cheek down on my head and we stood there for several moments, just holding onto each other.

I finally stepped back and turned to face Mikaela.

Shadow was now stretched out alongside her, much the way she'd been lying next to me. She made a mewing sound, and as if in response, Mikaela shifted into a giant leopard.

Shadow let out a happy, rumbling purr and set her head next to the giant leopard's head.

"I had no idea Mikaela was a leopard shifter," I said.

"She's half shifter, half witch, but she's never shifted before," Jasmine said. "Her magic manifested, but her leopard never appeared. That's the way it goes sometimes. You get one set of gifts, but not the other. Whatever happened to her must have woken her leopard with a vengeance."

I reached out and stroked Mikaela's head. Her fur was the same shade as her hair in human form. "You have to wake up, Mikaela."

Shadow let out a soft whimper.

"Where is everyone anyway?" I glanced around, surprised the nurse wasn't in here, fussing over Mikaela.

Jahrdran and Jasmine exchanged a look that had the hair on the nape of my neck standing up. "What? What's going on?"

"When I got back from getting snacks yesterday, you and Mikaela were gone," Jasmine said. "Then the alarms went off. A moment after that, you two came falling out of the closet."

"When the alarms went off," Jahrdran said, "all I could think of was getting to you."

"He came bursting into the dorm room and helped me carry you two here. Everyone thinks it was an intruder that set the alarms off," Jasmine said. "Then, when they realized how badly hurt Mikaela was, the whole castle went on lockdown."

"They're out at the docks right now," Jahrdran said, "trying to figure out if someone used the magical ferry without authorization, and if so, how to keep it from happening again."

"He didn't use the magical ferry," I said, staring down at Mikaela, remembering how she'd looked, completely relaxed, sprawled across the bed right before those damn shadows had wrapped around her. "He came straight from the shadow realm, just appeared in our dorm room."

Jahrdran blanched. "Who did?"

I just looked at him and he shook his head. "No. That's not possible. He should be dead. He *has* to be dead."

I hated to tell him what I was thinking, what I'd been thinking since we'd stood outside the library and eavesdropped, but he had to know. He had to prepare himself. "If the professors are right and he *wasn't* a shadow-beast, that means your people were never actually hunting the killer at all, so *yes*, he could still be alive."

"It's been two hundred years," he said desperately.

"And we were just attacked by the shadows," I told him.

Despair settled over his face and I stepped forward to hug him again. "It's all right. We'll figure it out."

"Please tell me you're not talking about who I think you are," Jasmine exclaimed.

I stepped back and looked up at Jahrdran.

He nodded, a resigned look on his face

I turned to face Jasmine. "It's the

Shadow Killer. He's back."

As if my words were some sort of prophetic announcement, the alarms went off again.

CHAPTER THIRTEEN

"JASMINE, STAY WITH Mikaela," I ordered as I ran toward the door of the infirmary.

Shadow, stay with them both.

"Where are you going?" Jasmine cried out after us.

It was a good question.

I froze just outside the door of the infirmary, uncertain of where to go, or if I *should* go anywhere at all.

MONSTER'S REWARD

Jahrdran stood behind me, one hand on my shoulder, telling me silently that wherever I went, he would be at my side.

But what if the Shadow Killer had come back for Mikaela?

I had just decided to go back into the infirmary when the screams began.

They weren't behind us.

We followed the screaming and the sounds of chaos through the halls to the main foyer.

Some students were shouting and panicking, while others, along with the professors, were casting spells, etching runes and flinging magic at streams of darkness that snaked through the foyer and up the staircase to higher levels, snatching students and professors and tossing them without fanfare into the shadows.

One student was grabbed from what looked like the third floor and was dropped, screaming.

I cringed in anticipation of the sound of her body breaking against the floor, but it didn't happen.

She fell into a shadow halfway down and was gone.

Professor Pulmeyer was using mirrors to dart in and around the shadow-tentacles, casting spells, trying to contain them, but she either didn't see one or miscalculated and was suddenly snatched up and flung into a shadow.

Seeing my professor launched so casually into the shadow realm somehow broke the paralysis that had kept me frozen, staring in shock at the chaos, and my shadow-beast lunged to the surface, roaring in rage.

For a split second, it was as if I was both human and shadows at the same time, then the human inside me just let everything go.

The fear that I was a monster destined to kill millions like the one whose actions had condemned my kind.

The iron control I kept on my shadows at all times, to never reveal my monster to my classmates.

My dread of them discovering what I was and condemning me for it.

I let it all go and everything that boiled inside me—the loneliness of being the last of my kind, the heartbreak at having my fated mate reject me and the rage at the execution order that had resulted in the genocide of all shadow-beasts everywhere—exploded free.

I became nothing but shadows and those shadows were one with the shadow realm.

I could somehow sense where my classmates and professors were—the Shadow Killer had claimed more than the ones I'd seen and he'd scattered them far and wide, yet I knew exactly where they were and sent my shadows chasing after them.

Then, it was as if my entire being was split in two as part of me raced through the shadow realm while the other part remained in the castle, monitoring the battle against the Shadow Killer.

I was peripherally aware of Headmistress Blackthorn and another group of professors arriving in a rush, magic exploding everywhere as they battled the Shadow Killer.

I also sensed the nurse and her assistants arriving and moving victims away from the foyer where the battle was taking place.

Most of my awareness, though, was split between the massive job of tracking the lost ones and monitoring Jahrdran as he hunted the Shadow Killer through the lower floors of the castle, undoubtedly hoping to stop the killer before he claimed more victims.

Meanwhile, my shadows went everywhere, thin ribbons of darkness and power snaking through the shadow realm, hunting the ones he'd already claimed, until finally, they found the ones they sought.

My shadows wrapped around my classmates and professors and *yanked* them all back at once, straight into the castle where they belonged.

The minute my shadows set them down, they all collapsed onto the floor, where they simply sat and watched as I pulled my shadows back in, then launched them out again.

The Shadow Killer was high above us now, at the very top of the castle, seeking more victims, though most had fled into their rooms.

Jahrdran was racing up the stairs, leaping from shadow to shadow, closing in on the fifth floor.

I saw the moment the Shadow Killer realized he was being hunted.

MONSTER'S REWARD

His shadows rolled down the staircase, heading directly for my mate.

Fury blazed inside as I wrapped my shadows around me, then launched us upward together.

The Shadow Killer must have sensed me coming, for his shadows dove off the stairs and barreled toward me.

We collided in an explosion of darkness somewhere near the fourth floor landing.

I heard Jahrdran's shout from somewhere above us, then sensed him hurtling toward us.

My heart about stopped when I realized he'd climbed over the stairwell and was free falling toward us, but then his shadows exploded from him in a wave of darkness—shadows, according to the book on shadow-mates, that were destined to come to all mates in time.

Several of those shadows reached us first, wrapping around the Shadow Killer as we grappled mid-air.

My shadows and Jahrdran's worked together, pouring over the Shadow Killer, wrapping tighter and tighter around him.

Then, our shadows in perfect sync, we yanked the Shadow Killer with us toward the floor.

We spiraled downward, in a tangle of shadows

Then, something exploded in my face, slapping me back so hard my shadows contracted back inside me and I was in my human form, falling.

At the last moment, shadows

wrapped around me again and I was yanked into Jahrdran's arms, his shadows cradling me close.

Above us, the Shadow Killer bared his fangs and roared.

His shadows had also retreated and he was now in his human form, but he hadn't fallen because he had wings that were as dark as night keeping him afloat.

Wings, I realized, that had exploded from him when we were falling, that had slapped me back and yanked him free.

All I felt in that moment was a sort of giddy relief that he was *not* a shadow-beast, though I wasn't sure what he was.

Gargoyle?

Dark elf?

Something else?

I reached deep and dragged my shadows forward again.

This time it hurt when I launched them out.

They were weak and tired and so was I.

Still, I managed to catch his foot with one tentacle and yanked him toward me.

He got close enough I could see the fury in his eyes, which were dark and boiled with shadows, before he simply ripped himself free.

"I got a taste of your little leopard friend and her fiery magic," he hissed. "She was delicious. When she wakes and discovers the gifts I left her, tell her I'll be coming for her." He grinned. "I'll be coming for her and then for you, my little shadow-beast."

MONSTER'S REWARD

Jahrdran let out a roar and lunged around me, but the shadow killer simply darted back with a laugh, then pulled his wings tight to his body before flinging them out again.

They exploded into writhing shadows that yanked him away, almost faster than I could follow.

He hurtled into the shadows beneath the staircase and was gone.

I sagged against Jahrdran, who carefully lowered us to the floor, where he cradled me against his chest, arms wrapped around me from behind.

The sound of heels approached, then a shadow fell over us.

I slowly tilted my head back and saw it was Headmistress Blackthorn who stood, staring down at us, hands on her hips. "Ms. Smith," she said sternly, "impressive control of your shadow-beast. Very impressive indeed." She gave one firm nod, then turned and walked away, leaving silence in her wake.

A moment later, the whispers exploded around us, "She's a shadow monster."

"Shadow-beast, the headmistress said," someone corrected.

I sighed.

One freaking moment and now I was exposed to the entire damn school.

"Well, Kasi, I see you've finally mastered the ability to yank people where you'd like them to go." I glanced up and found Professor Dewar standing over me, Verity cradled in her arms. "Though I'm also beginning to understand why you were reluctant to do so on a non-emergency basis."

I winced.

I hadn't fully registered it at the time, but I now realized that Professor Dewar had also been in the shadow realm when I yanked everyone free.

"It *was* quite the dramatic way of transporting someone," Professor Pulmeyer agreed as she joined us. "I think I prefer the mirrors, myself, but I am grateful, my dear, for the save. I'll see you in class tomorrow." She turned and walked away.

"I'm quite grateful as well," Professor Dewar said. "Verity is even more so, since she would have been left all alone had you not come after me."

I nodded. "I'm glad she's okay. I didn't

sense her in the shadow realm with you."

"No. She happened to be across the room when the shadows grabbed me. I trust *your* Shadow is also safe," Despite her words, she had a worried look on her face, proving once and for all, that while Shadow might be scary to some, for cat people, she was simply another cat to be adored.

I smiled up at her. "She's in the infirmary, keeping Mikaela and Jasmine company. Shadow helped me find Mikaela and save her, you know."

Professor Dewar nodded, then laid a hand on Verity's head, carefully covering her ears before leaning forward. "I think I shall knit her a hat for her bravery, but don't tell Verity." Without waiting for a reply, she turned and walked away.

"I'm not sure Shadow will appreciate her efforts," Jahrdran observed.

I snickered. "She'll have it shredded in two minutes, guaranteed, and if Verity sees the hat before it's destroyed, well, the rivalry between the cats will reach new and unparalleled heights."

Jahrdran chuckled, then rose to his feet and held his hand out to me. "Come on. Let's go see how Mikaela's faring."

I set my hand in his and let him pull me to my feet.

The journey back to the infirmary took quite some time as both students and professors kept stopping us, some to thank me for pulling them out of the shadow realm and others simply out of curiosity, wanting to speak to the only shadow-beast in existence.

"Do you realize who that monster was?" One of Jahrdran's classmates, a dragon named Elliot, stopped us to ask.

I shook my head. "Not a clue."

"He's a chameleon dragon, like me," Elliot said. "They're super rare, able to take on the characteristics of those around them to blend in. Did you notice how his wings were as black as night?"

I nodded.

"They were blending with the shadows."

"They *were* the shadows," I said. "Even when he was in human form, they didn't look fully solid, especially at the end, when they just exploded into shadows and dragged him away."

"It's the gift of the chameleon, but it's

dangerous too," Elliot said. "If you absorb too much of whatever's around you and then fail to shake it off, you can lose yourself in the camouflage. Based on what I just saw, his wings are probably more shadow than real now, especially if he's been in the shadows for as long as I suspect he has."

"How long do you think he's been in there?" Jahrdran asked.

"A couple hundred years, maybe more. He's got to be about three hundred by now. He was mated to a shadow-beast who died."

"How do you know all this?" I asked.

"I've seen his picture in family photos. He was my father's best friend, once upon a time. Then his mate died and my dad never really saw him after that. I honestly thought he was dead. If his fated mate died, he *should* be dead."

"And because he isn't, he's been killing millions for hundreds of years," I said.

"Wait. You think he was the Shadow Killer?" Elliot asked.

"You saw what he did in there, right?" Jahrdran asked.

"Well, yeah, but—" He shook his head. "I can't believe it's been a dragon all this time. Maybe I just don't *want* to believe it."

I had to bite my tongue to keep from saying what I was thinking, that my people had died because a dragon had gone on a rampage, which meant the dragons owed their lives to the shadow-beasts.

That wasn't fair, though, and Elliot certainly didn't deserve my anger.

There was nothing to be done about the past, and there was still a shadow killer on the loose, one who knew how to infiltrate the Academy, who knew there were two students there capable of hunting him in the shadows, and who intended to come after Mikaela and me again.

I had much more important things to worry about than a past I could not change.

CHAPTER FOURTEEN

WE SPENT THE evening in the infirmary—Jasmine, Jahrdran, Shadow, and me.

And Mikaela, of course.

Though she didn't wake that night or any night thereafter for the rest of the semester.

As for Jahrdran and me, we had our growing pains, as we learned to trust one another again, but in the end, we were stronger than ever.

It helped that everyone now knew the truth.

Headmistress Blackthorn had made certain to share with the Varulvka Council a recording of the events at the Academy, showing the battle with the Shadow Killer in its entirety.

This meant the Varulvka Council knew that I existed and that my mate was one of them.

They also knew the true Shadow Killer was a chameleon dragon named Lydrel Zowen, a shadow-mate, but not himself a shadow-beast, and that he had served as ambassador for the Council of Shadows.

The truth had exploded like a bomb across the supernatural community, causing upheaval and mayhem as the myth of the shadow-beasts came into the light of day and the entire world learned of their tragic end.

Jahrdran and all of the Varulvka struggled to reconcile who they believed they were as a community, with the reality of what their ancestors had done.

Talk of monuments honoring those fallen had been discussed, as had reparations, but no one knew how to make them when there was no one left, but me, to represent the victims, and I wanted nothing to do with their reparations.

They could make them all they wanted, but nothing would bring back the dead.

In the end, all any of us could do was

move forward and try to do better.

The best part of the truth coming out was that the oath died with it. Because the oath had been extremely specific, naming the Shadow Killer a shadow-beast and condemning all shadow-beasts as a result, the moment the truth came to light that the Shadow Killer was in fact, a chameleon dragon, *not* a shadow-beast, the oath simply disintegrated and the Varulvka were free from its demands.

The worst part about the truth coming out, though, was that everyone at school now knew what I was, which made it much more difficult to hide in the shadows.

The professors all began insisting that I physically appear in class, rather than texting from them.

My classmates took their cue from our professors and began inviting me to sit with them at meals, to accompany them to Wellspring for a night on the town and to join them for study sessions.

My days of being forgotten were long gone.

Shadow, of course, accompanied me everywhere, and even let the students see her every now and then.

Best of all, she was now allowed to participate in Familiar Training with me, which was a lot more enjoyable.

Even so, Professor Dewar insisted I continue our private lessons as well. I think she just enjoyed the extra time with Shadow, not that she'd ever admit it with Verity around.

Professor Dewar also kept her promise and presented Shadow with a hat made just for her.

It was truly hideous, a combination of grays and blacks, so that it blended with Shadow's smoky appearance. There were two holes at the top for her ears to poke through and it had two long braids, one on either side, so that when Shadow got to running super fast, they would stream behind her in a long wave.

I'd been absolutely certain that Shadow would eat the hat within minutes, but apparently tormenting Verity was of higher priority than destroying the ugliest hat I'd ever seen.

This was because Verity took one look at that hat, and decided it should be hers. This resulted in many cat shenanigans as Verity chased Shadow around the gardens, lunging for her head.

Eventually, they would wear themselves out and every once in a while, we'd glance over to discover they'd curled up in the grass together and were fast asleep.

As my second year at the Academy drew to a close, the tension in the castle rose, not only because final exams were approaching, but also because we were all waiting for the other shoe to drop.

Zowen—I refused to call him the Shadow Killer now that we knew his true name—had not attacked again and no one was certain why.

We speculated, of course.

Maybe he'd been hurt and was regaining his strength, though I couldn't imagine it would take this long. After all, the shadows healed shadow-beasts *and* their mates.

Maybe he was simply torturing us, waiting for us to let our guard down, so that his next attack would take us by surprise.

Or perhaps he was waiting on Mikaela, whose parents had taken her home the moment the doctors deemed her stable enough for transport.

It was the last possibility that caused me the greatest concern.

I feared Mikaela would never wake up, or if she did, that she would not be allowed to return to Blackthorn Academy.

Worse, I feared if she did return, Zowen would attack her again.

The Headmistress, the dean of students and all the professors had warded the entire castle again and had even attempted to ward the shadows themselves against intruders.

I could have told them it was an impossible task.

Shadows moved minute by minute.

They were there one day and not the next.

Attempting to ward them, then, seemed a futile effort.

As I listened to the professors argue over how best to protect the castle, I finally understood the desperation everyone must have felt two hundred years before when they realized the futility of attempting to stop a shadow-beast from trespassing wherever they wanted.

I still couldn't quite condone it, but I did understand.

They'd been desperate for a solution as millions had died and they'd taken the one they felt had the highest chance of success.

It didn't make it right, but I did understand.

The night I came to that epiphany was a turning point for Jahrdran and me.

Though we were together again and he stayed every night with me under my bed, we'd only been sleeping there.

He could barely look at me some days, the shame was so intense around him, and though I wanted to help, I was struggling with my own issues.

I was bitter and angry and worried about Mikaela, so it was hard for me to look at Jahrdran and not blame him, too.

For a while, we didn't speak much, just went to classes during the day, ate our evening meals with Jasmine and our classmates, then held each other tight through the nights.

Then, one evening when I was feeling pretty raw about Mikaela still not waking, I came upon the scene in the main foyer where the Headmistress was leading the rest of the staff in a complicated weave that was intended to ward the shadows of the Academy.

I simply stood there, in one of those

shadows they were trying to ward, and watched as they did their best to protect the students in their care.

In the end, they were satisfied with their efforts and left, feeling pleased with themselves, that they'd managed to at least add another layer of protection over the castle.

I let them have their moment of triumph, for there was no sense in bursting their bubble and causing a panic.

In the end, either Zowen would come for me or he would not.

Perhaps I should offer to leave the Academy to keep everyone safe, but this was literally the only home I'd ever really known and I wasn't willing to give it up.

Not until I had to anyway.

PEPPER MCGRAW

I returned to our room that evening and crawled into Jahrdran's arms.

We lay beneath my bed in silence as we had for the majority of the semester while I gathered my thoughts.

"You need to let go of the guilt and the shame," I said softly into the dark, safely wrapped in his arms, my head on his chest, listening to the beat of his heart. "You're not to blame for what your ancestors did. Let go of the guilt and shame and I'll let go of my anger and my bitterness."

"How can you even offer that?" His voice was gravelly and rough. "You *should* be angry and bitter. Your people were slaughtered for no reason. And *my* people did it."

"Because my anger and bitterness

will destroy me if I'm not careful. Worse, they'll destroy us *and* our mate bond. So I have to let them go—for me, for you, for *us.*

"I'm begging you, Jahrdran. Please, do the same."

He shook in my arms. "I don't know if I can."

"Of course, you can." I leaned up to stare into his eyes. I cradled his cheeks in the palms of my hand and rested my forehead against his. "I'm here with you, loving you, *needing* you. To be here in the moment with me, Jahrdran, all you have to do is *let them go."*

He shook his head, shoulders shaking as a tear slid from one gorgeous, blue eye.

I caught the tear with my finger,

smoothing it away, then kissed his cheek, his jawline, his lips.

"I love you, Jahrdran," I murmured against his lips. "Love me enough to let it go."

His arms wrapped around me in a compulsive move and he buried his face in my neck.

I rolled us over so that he was on top, then cradled him close as my sweet monster mate broke into a million pieces in my arms, then allowed me to put him back together again.

When the storm had passed, he lifted his head to stare in my eyes again. "Can you really forgive me?"

"There's nothing to forgive, Jahrdran. Unless, of course, we're talking about how you rejected me—not once, but twice, mind you—then, well." I shrugged and grinned up at him. "I have to think about it."

He chuckled, the sound and vibration of it rumbling through me, then sobered. "You joke, but I truly am sorry, my love." He leaned down and kissed me slowly. "You're everything to me and you cannot imagine the strength of will it took to walk away, but I just couldn't trust that I wouldn't give in to the oath at any moment and kill the one I loved more than life itself."

I blinked back tears, stunned.

It had never really occurred to me that he was rejecting me to protect me, but it should have. A tiny, still hurt piece of me began to heal in that moment. "I love you, Jahrdran."

"Ah, sweet Kasi mine. I love you, too, and I am grateful every single day that the fates believed I deserved a mate such as you." He captured my lips in a searing kiss, then murmured against my lips. "I cannot imagine what I did to earn such an exquisite reward, but I am truly blessed."

"I'm your reward, am I?"

"You are."

I shook my head. "I think you have it backward. After all the loneliness and sorrow, after being left alone for so long, the last of my people in an unkind world, I think *you* are *my* reward."

"Perhaps, my love, we shall be each other's."

I smiled up at him. "I like that. Very much. Now claim me. Claim me again, so all will know that I am yours and you are mine and nothing will tear us apart ever again."

"Kasi," he rumbled, then took my lips in a kiss so scorching hot, every thought was obliterated as heat rolled over us in a massive wave.

We clutched at each other, struggling to remove our clothes and get closer, skin-to-skin.

We rolled ourselves from beneath my bed right into the shadow realm, where the shadows enveloped us, blanketing our bodies in joyous welcome.

Shadow came bounding out of the dark and bounced around us happily a couple times, making me giggle and Jahrdran let out a rumble of impatience.

One final leap over us and Shadow

raced away again, probably off to chase some shadow mice or something like that.

"Kasima, my love," Jahrdran murmured, lowering his head to kiss me once more. His tongue plunged deep, sending waves of heat barreling through me.

"Jahrdran," I whispered, kissing him back, clutching at his shoulders, scratching my nails down his back as he ever so slowly pushed his way inside.

I'd forgotten how good this felt—how good *he* felt.

More, I'd somehow forgotten how incredibly *huge* he was, taking up all the space and then some, to the point of pain, as he pressed forward, never stopping.

His cock slowly dragged along my insides, lighting them on fire as he sank deep.

Finally, finally, he bottomed out and we hung there, the two of us, holding our breath on a precipice as my pussy rippled around him.

"Ah, sweet Kasi," he groaned above me. "Hold on."

I wrapped my arms around him as he pulled back, then powered forward.

I inhaled, then cried out as he repeated the motion, dragging his cock forward and back, hitting a sweet spot inside over and over again, one that lit me up and made me cry out every time he rubbed over it.

Oh, fuck.

"Jahrdran, Jahrdran, *please!*"

He just grunted, slid his hands beneath my bottom, lifting me as he levered himself up onto his knees and increased the power of every thrust, rubbing over that same sweet spot, this time from a different angle, one that sent me headlong off a cliff.

I didn't even have time to catch my breath before I was sent barreling into a second orgasm and then a third.

He powered into me over and over again, until all I could feel was him, all I could hear were his grunts and my breathless cries and all I could see were his beautiful eyes as they stared into mine while he drove me up and over the precipice again and again and again.

"Jahrdran!"

EPILOGUE

Mikaela

MY BODY FELT strange, as if my skin was pulled too tight, and beneath its surface, monsters roiled.

I tried to open my eyes, but they were heavy, sealed shut.

I drifted.

Lost.

Trapped.

There was no urgency or sense of time passing, just the quiet and the dark.

Until a spark became a flame.

And the flame turned into an inferno that unleashed an avalanche of memories.

Who I was.

What I was.

The magic I held deep inside.

I reached for that power.

The embers that have always lived inside me were now a seething, boiling cauldron of flames that leapt and snapped and lashed out from my core.

They were no longer just made up of fire, though.

Ice now spread along their edges, freezing some of those outer flames, while something else writhed at their center.

Shadows.

PEPPER MCGRAW

Shadows and a darkness I wished I did not remember, that I hoped never to experience again.

Something scraped deep, raking across the inside of my skin like an itch I could never reach or scratch.

The sensation pulled my attention away from the flames and dragged it toward whatever it was that crawled beneath my skin and roared for freedom.

Crouched at the very back of my mind, as far from the flames as she could get, a leopard snarled, tail swishing back and forth in agitation.

My leopard.

I held out my hand and tried to coax her closer.

It's okay, I whispered. *We're going to be okay. I'm so happy you're here.*

She simply snarled in response.

Thank you for trying to protect me.

No answer.

I inched closer, still holding out my hand.

The leopard hissed, then exploded into shadows and disappeared.

I leapt forward, trying to follow, and landed in my own bed, wide awake, the sound of my leopard's snarl ringing in my ears.

Thank you for reading this installation of the Blackthorn Academy for Supernaturals shared world!

Don't miss Mikaela's story in Monster's Madness.

www.peppermcgraw.com/blackthorn-academy

Read the next book in the series now!

Watch for the other books in the
Blackthorn Academy for Supernaturals
shared world series.

Monster's Kiss

Monster's Delight

Monster's Spell

Monster's Enemy

Monster's Past

Monster's Secret

Monster's Magic

Monster's Reward

Monster's Obsession

Monster's Mayhem

Monster's Bride

Monster's Charm

and More!

FOLLOW PEPPER MCGRAW

Sign up for Pepper's newsletter and get a free story...

www.peppermcgraw.com/newsletter

www.peppermcgraw.com

www.bookbub.com/authors/pepper-mcgraw

www.facebook.com/groups/matchmakingcatsofthegoddesses

www.facebook.com/ShenanigansSeries

www.facebook.com/groups/theshenanigancrew

www.tiktok.com/@peppermcgraw

www.twitter.com/peppermcgraw

If you enjoyed this book, you may also enjoy...

A Pawsitively Purrfect Match
The Cat's Meow

Holly Jolly Pawliday

Hocus Purrcus

Tridents & Tails

Abra-Cat-Abra

Satan's Kitty

Her Dark Obsession

Valen-Cats

Shenanigans:
Crazed

Amazed

Holidazed

Stories of the Veil
Guardians of the Veil

MONSTER'S REWARD

ABOUT PEPPER MCGRAW

Pepper is a USA Today Bestselling Author of paranormal romance. Her life to date has sadly been paranormal-free, but she knows it's simply a matter of time before her fated mate finally appears. Until that glorious day arrives, she keeps herself busy writing (and reading) paranormal romances.

Pepper is a huge fan of all animals, but is especially fond of cats, and spends her free time volunteering at local shelters and for Trap-Neuter-Release programs. She's had the supreme honor of winning occasional head butts and meows from the local ferals in her neighborhood and has even convinced a few to come inside and adopt her as their own.